Penguin Books
Double-Barrel

Since his birth in the Gray's Inn Road in the borough of St
Pancras, Nicolas Freeling has lived all his days in Europe.
Fifteen years as a cook in expensive, and generally nasty,
restaurants: thereafter, novelist. His house lies on a historic
route from Germany through to France. It has been most
things, and now has a future as a lighthouse. *Love in
Amsterdam*, his first novel, was published in 1962, closely
followed by his second and third novels, *Because of the Cats*
and *Gun before Butter*, which were published in 1963. His
other crime novels include *Valparaiso, Criminal Conversation,
The King of the Rainy Country, The Dresden Green, Strike
Out Where Not Applicable, This is the Castle, Tsing-Boum,
Over the High Side, A Long Silence, Dressing of Diamond,
What are the Bugles Blowing for?, Lake Isle, Gadget, The
Night Lords, The Widow, One Damn Thing After Another,
Castang's City, Wolfnight, Back of the North Wind* and *No
Part in Your Death*. Many of these are published in Penguins.

Nicolas Freeling

# Double-Barrel

Penguin Books

PENGUIN BOOKS

Published by the Penguin Group
Penguin Books Ltd, 27 Wrights Lane, London W8 5TZ, England
Viking Penguin, a division of Penguin Books USA Inc.
375 Hudson Street, New York, New York 10014, USA
Penguin Books Australia Ltd, Ringwood, Victoria, Australia
Penguin Books Canada Ltd, 2801 John Street, Markham, Ontario, Canada L3R 1B4
Penguin Books (NZ) Ltd, 182–190 Wairau Road, Auckland 10, New Zealand

Penguin Books Ltd, Registered Offices: Harmondsworth, Middlesex, England

First published in the United States by Harper & Row Publishers, Inc., New York 1964
Published by Penguin Books Inc. by arrangement with Harper & Row, Publishers, Inc.
First published in Great Britain by Victor Gollancz 1964
Published in Penguin Books 1967
10 9 8 7 6 5 4

Printed in England by Clays Ltd, St Ives plc
Set in Monotype Times

# Part one: 'Happenstance'

# 1

How often it happens. We imagine some situation, or even construct a whole hypothetical case in the course of a discussion. It may be serious – it might be just said as a joke. But next week it comes true. There is something laughable about that even when the reality is disagreeable.

Back in the office, I did laugh, but the irreverence might have been to offset a strong idea that the next few weeks would be unpleasant. It was ridiculous, and from this far away it was fairly funny – but it was sinister, it was horrible, and it was certainly tragic.

There it was. I had gone and theorized, all pompous. And today my hypothesis gets presented to me complete in every detail.

A lot of good my theorizing will do me now. As likely as not I am going to fall straight on my classic, scornful nose.

It is my wife's fault. I am not unhappy that Arlette is French; it helps me often enough to remember not to be quite so Dutch when I try to understand things. After twelve years she is still rebellious about Holland, and sometimes uneasy there. She won't surrender to some of the attitudes natural to any Dutch woman, with their generations behind them of what she calls their conditioned reflex. The phrase is not all that bad. It sounds like Mr Pavlov's dogs, and there is a good deal in common.

It was not even a week ago; evening. She was reading the paper and I was sitting in my socks, majestically doing nothing, probably with the socks on the coffee-table where

I could admire their intricate beauty; grey wool, three and eleven in the January sales that were just over. The wall of newsprint opposite gave an indignant crackle. A voice said, 'Pah!'

'What is pah?' No great interest; just making a sympathetic sound.

'An advertisement for washing powder. In a headline, sub-heading, and five lines of text, the word "Fresh" is repeated six times. S-I-X.'

'Ach. Every time they want to sell something to a housewife they tell her how fresh it will make her grey existence.'

'But six times . . .'

'It's a witchword. Everything approved of in Holland is fresh, whether it's the kitchen floor or a pretty girl.'

Snort from Arlette.

'I only buy things from now on that are unfresh.'

'Ha. I read a film review the other day; the sort of film – you know, takes the lid off the call-girl industry. Described by the reviewer as "decidedly unfresh" – you could see him holding his nose.'

'I wish to go and see it immediately.'

'I wonder what he'd call my daily life.'

'Not as fresh as we would like.'

I got an idea, with a mild galvanic effect that aimed my feet towards the bookshelf. A book I have annotated. The annotations are probably silly, but I think about Louis XVIII, writing little notes in the margin of his Horace while Napoleon was on his way from Elba. Van der Valk being civilized while Amsterdam wallows in unfresh crime. Poor fellow; he's tired.

'You don't understand Holland. Listen – this is Stendhal, talking about the America of eighteen twenty. Meaning puritan New England, a hundred years after the Salem witch-trials. Where am I? – yes – "The physical gaiety of Americans disappears as they reach twenty. A habit of reason, of caution, of prudence, makes love impossible."

What does that remind you of? – he cites, by the way, a mental climate hostile to art or literature.'

'It does sound like Holland.'

'Or this – describing a love affair in Protestant North Germany. "The sun is pale in Halberstadt, the government very particular and these two personages pretty cold. In the most passionate tête-à-tête, Kant and Klopstock are always present."'

'Giggle as you like – I don't think it funny.'

'Be glad you live in Amsterdam. Think of living in a provincial town in Drente, and discovering that murder was a crime, right enough, but falling asleep during the sermon a lot worse.'

'Is that the worst crime?'

'I think that making love to your own wife in the living-room in the middle of the afternoon will count as the most serious.'


# 2

I was in the office on the Marnixstraat next morning, unravelling a long wearisome report about a bank fraud. Holland is a strange country. Every single thing is fragmented, organized, and subject to a thick book of rules, and here was the treasurer of a large concern happily speculating with thousands that weren't his – undetected or even suspected for years. He looked, you see, so utterly respectable, and the rules were such gobbledygook that nobody could understand them anyway without three diplomas for treasuring. Phone buzzed. My superior, Commissaris Tak of Central Recherche. An old maid if ever I saw one.

'Van der Valk? The Procureur-Général wants to see you. Right away.'

'Oh lord, what have I done wrong now?'

'Nothing, as far as I know.'

'What's it about?'

'I haven't been told. You'd better get over to the Prinsengracht and find out, hadn't you.'

I put my jacket on. Central heating was too hot today. Real February; westerly, windy, rainy. Not cold, but here that does not mean that winter is now over. It'll probably be snowing tomorrow.

'Nice and fresh,' my colleague said coming in this morning. We share a room – there is space for the two of us, our papers, and maybe one beer bottle, carefully concealed behind a report on the number of auto thefts there were in nineteen thirty-eight.

It is five minutes' walk to the Palace of Justice, and I spent them wondering what I would get the telling-off for. The Procureur-Général is a most important personage. He is supposed to be busy presenting appeal cases to the Court of Cassation or whatnot, or codifying public morals, but he has a trick of finding time to censure imprudences of unimportant functionaries – and that has meant me, more than once.

There is a barrier of pale legal advisers to penetrate before one reaches the sanctuary where the big Boums contemplate pale legal paper in utter silence. Here the telephone lines are all guarded, and probably the lowest typist is under some awful oath – Safety of the Realm Act 1823.

At least in the other half of this big building it is more human. There sits the 'Parquet' – the prosecutors, the Officers of Justice and the Children's Court – and policemen sit on benches with criminals in an atmosphere of almost-cordiality. Over here, the milk-of-human-kindness has been in the autoclave. Well and truly sterile.

I reached a secretary; elderly soul with prim blue hair and no lips.

'Inspector van der Valk, on the instructions of Commissaris Tak.'

An approving nod for that. She picked up the intercom phone and spoke in hushed tones. The Vatican voice. Cardinal commanding the Holy Office here.

'Will you please go straight in?'

Master Anthoni Sailer, learned in the law, is a tall dry man, a bit creaky. Body, nose, lip: all long and perfectly straight. The straight hair combed across a high white forehead to hide a balding patch is still dark. His look is direct – yes, straight. And his handwriting is upright and always legible, in black ink with a fine pen. But he is capable of understanding. Even, as I once learned during an otherwise unpleasant interview, capable of humour. Acid: arid – but humour.

'Ah – Van der Valk. Sit down, then.' He took a horizon-blue folder from the side of his desk, opened it, arranged it perfectly parallel to the edge of his blotter, and studied the opening paragraph of the contents. Short pause, legal but pregnant, giving me time to wonder what it was pregnant with.

'I have been posed an unusual problem, and after thought I have reached an unusual conclusion. Incidentally, have you ever been in Drente?'

'No, sir.'

'I am thinking of sending you there.'

Big fright. I had a sudden vision of Louis XV saying in his icy voice, 'Monsieur Maurepas, you will retire immediately to your estate in the country.' Damn it, I'll resign first.

'It would amount to a temporary detachment, upon a temporary duty. An unusual duty, and delicate. Demanding tact as well as ability. Naturally you may refuse if you wish; it is not an order. But first you must study this folder.'

Leisurely, Master Sailer drew a little tube of throat pastilles from his breast pocket and popped one with dignity behind his wisdom tooth. There was a minute twitch, but not by a millimetre did it bulge the straight-shaved cheek.

'I have upon occasion,' slowly, 'criticized your handling of circumstances. And I have had occasion to praise your – penetration. Since this affair calls for just that quality, I am asking you to use it – but with more discretion than you have been known to show.'

'Thank you, sir.'

'Among the officers of police within my jurisdiction, I thought of you.'

'Thank you, sir.'

'You would have, consequently, the complete confidence and support of the relevant authorities. Possessing that confidence, this support, you are capable of justifying my choice. As I estimate.'

'Thank you, sir.'

'Good. Drente, you are doubtless thinking, is not within my jurisdiction. This problem is now over six months old. It has – baffled is not too strong – the local municipal police of a small town called Zwinderen, and an inspector from Assen, and became subsequently the subject of inquiry by the State Recherche officers, who have produced a file of exhaustive investigation with little positive result. The file finally reached my colleague in Leeuwarden, who has sent it to me for study and possible comment. His conclusion was that a man from the city – with, that is to say, no local connexions or even knowledge – may overcome the apparent obstacles. I am prepared, conditional to your acceptance, to advise him that you may be the man for his task.'

What answer could one make to that?

'I will now give you the relevant parts of this dossier for study.'

'Can I take them home?'

'Files here don't get taken home. They get studied here; they don't leave this building. There is a small room where you will be undisturbed. Take the whole morning if you wish. I shall inform Mr Tak that I am holding you at my disposal. Come back when you have decided. You will have to consider whether you believe yourself competent to succeed where these other gentlemen' – with a sudden gleam – 'got stuck in the bog.'

All I know about Drente is that it is up in the north-east corner of Holland, between Groningen and the German border. A poor province; the ground is not much good for agriculture. Wet, peaty sort of moorland. What in Ireland is called 'the bog'. Oh!

It had taken me nearly five minutes to see that Sailer had made a joke.

Rather flabbergasted, I was led to a small menacing room, and the photostat girl brought me a cup of legal coffee. After reading the first twenty pages of general introductory remarks I gave a sort of moan. Why hadn't Arlette kept her mouth shut?

Twenty pages further I was thinking that this affair was a bit unfresh too. And that, doubtless, is why everybody seems to have thought of Van der Valk.

3

'Well?'

'Well, sir – I mean yes, sir. I accept, of course. May I state a few brief conclusions? Better say a few steps that I think it would be necessary to take?'

'Certainly.'

'There's been a lot of policemen. One more, and he won't get anywhere at all – more likely to get his eye blackened. I believe, sir, that if I go at all it should not be as a policeman. Am I allowed to make a suggestion?'

'Yes.'

'A state functionary, with some foolproof cover to explain the nosing about and questioning. A – a – I don't know – inspector of tax dividends or something. I think that nobody should know who or what I am.'

Thought. Dought. Sorry doubt. Reconsideration. Conclusion.

'The point is well taken. The burgomaster will have to know. You will be responsible to him – but to him alone – and can make a direct verbal report. But this – cover. I think I can agree and I think I could arrange it.' Weird but indubitable legal smile. 'How would you like to be an official – a responsible official – of the Ministry of the Interior? That is not, technically, an untruth. Shall we say that such an official might be sent from The Hague to draw up a detailed report on aspects of a provincial town. Perhaps with a view to the further industrial expansion in a district of underdevelopment? Mm, your powers of inquiry should be very broad and extremely vague. I am casting about for a suitable vague, impressive, minatory phrase ... Suppose we were to say that you were conducting Ethnographic Research? That means nothing and will cover everything.'

Really, he has understood. I have to be able to blind the tiny local bigwigs with bullshit.

'I dislike conspiracies, but this is an unorthodox situation. It is justifiable to meet it in an unorthodox way,' meditating. 'I have no doubt but that you can be provided with a lodging, transport, an identity, as well as various necessary papers.' Very cool indeed.

He reached for the private-line telephone.

'Will you please get me the Minister of the Interior at The Hague? ... There is a further point' – while his call was winging towards another discreet burr in another padded, panelled office – 'I should like you to be accompanied by your wife. You may be there some time, and if you are to be the complete, convincing, colourless if intelligent state functionary, you need a wife to do the housekeeping.'

'My wife is French, sir.'

'Better a French wife than none at all,' remarked Mr Sailer charmingly. 'Ah – Good morning, Excellency . . .'

# 4

A week later I had a black Volkswagen and a new identity, supported by most impressive and not-quite-totally incomprehensible papers. I was making a preliminary survey of Zwinderen, a small market town rapidly growing past the fifteen thousand persons mark, in the extreme north-eastern corner of the province of Drente, a scant twenty kilometres from the German border. As an official introduction to this new sphere, I had an appointment with the burgomaster.

A modern town hall, very large for a place this size. Very ugly for anywhere. Lot of money and all wasted. The steps were very grand, where the couples stand to be photographed after being married, the farmers' sons vastly uneasy in hired top hats. You don't even get married by the mayor with his sash on, in Holland. It's done by a character whose title is 'Functionary of the Civil Status' – there's nothing more Dutch than that. The steps of the town hall have to be pretty grand to make up for it. But Holland can be nice. There are tiny dorps in Friesland that were places of importance in the sixteenth century, with perhaps five thousand souls now, but possessing magnificent Renaissance and baroque town halls, their façades towering and curling above sleepy tiny squares, and steps . . . like Napoleon taking leave of the Old Guard at Fontainebleau.

Inside, black-and-white rubber marble. Aseptic corridors, with glass sliding windows to protect the functionary from the contagious, coughing public. Various depressed members of the said public, waiting to be noticed and

14

kindly to be allowed to register a child's birth – but only if the name is approved of by the Handbook for Functionaries of the Civil Status. And finally a light, airy, freshly-painted office.

The burgomaster got up from his desk when a neat and competent-seeming female showed me in. He had a firm, resilient face; quite the portrait of a burgomaster. He could hang later in some pompous frame, looking down benignly on the couples getting married. Not quite on the same wall as the swimmy-sentimental portraits of royalty, but well up there in the league – presented by a grateful municipality after he retired, handsome and silver-haired. But he did not look a nonentity. I had already decided anyway that he would not be a dud – this was the man in charge of a town scheduled for expansion into a thriving industrial community. In twenty years there would be sixty thousand people here; it was already well on the way and it was his work.

'Good morning, burgomaster.'

'Good morning; pleased to make your acquaintance.' He turned to the secretary, waiting with an alert, impersonal face. 'Accessible to no one; I am in conference.'

'Very good, burgomaster.' The door shut crisply.

'I have an hour. Sit down, Mr van der Valk; let us get to know each other – and see what we can do for each other.'

An hour later I had a lot. Access to everything; neat dockets of disturbing information in close detail; assurance of every co-operation; a hearty handshake, and a request for a verbal report twice a week at least – at his home; that would be more discreet. No need to let the municipal officials into our little secret. I was an embarrassment; he would prefer to see as little as possible of me officially. I could see how he disliked this hole-and-corner game – but he had been convinced of its necessity.

I got passed to the secretary, who was helpful. I had been wondering where on earth I was going to be lodged, and

15

what the point of the wife was. Now I found that the wheels had turned, and the hand of the Procureur-Général had reached as far as this tiny tentacle of central government.

'I have been instructed, Mr van der Valk' – bright, very efficient and both conscious and proud of it – 'that you will be staying here a few weeks. You'll be glad to hear that I've a furnished house for you – oh, only a little one, but at least you'll be independent of hotels. You see, we do quite often have to house officials: inspectors, headmasters; people whose own houses and belongings aren't yet ready. Or of course people who are here temporarily, as in your case; we've had functionaries from The Hague before, doing these administrative surveys. I'm afraid the furniture is rather a scratch lot, but it's adequate. The house does tend to look as though it had no owner – well, of course, it hasn't. I do hope your wife will be comfortable – but if there's any little thing you or she need, you've only to ask me. Any help – I'm delighted if I can be of service.'

Simple as that. In another week, I would be installed, with Arlette and several suitcases, in the Mimosastraat in Zwinderen, province of Drente. Access to everything. I had already arranged for the children to be boarded out, in the house of Inspector and Mrs Suykerland of the Amsterdamse Police. They would get frightful food, but they were delighted with the notion. It all sounded like a holiday. All I had to do was clear up an affair that had not only baffled a lot of people just as intelligent as me, but that had also been trodden on by so many big boots full of flat feet as to be nearly illegible.

# 5

I had already been relieved of all ordinary duties – Mr Tak was cross but floored by a minatory letter from the Prinsengracht. By the time we moved, I had spent six days studying – but on paper, only on paper – the life of Zwinderen, which when I went to school had been an ossified tiny market town away in the wilds, a stone's throw from Protestant North Germany; but now was become the frontier of the big push at decentralization, decongestion, full employment and Prosperity for All. Boom town. Light industry and housing. Practically Dodge City.

I was Wyatt Earp, getting sent there as United States Marshal. I had better start polishing my forty-five and practising quick draws.

The keyword in this north-eastern corner of Holland is 'Veen'. It occurs as a suffix in place-names. Over to the west are Hoogeveen and Heerenveen – larger towns these, around the twenty thousand mark. To the south, Klazinaveen, Vriezeveen – smaller, hardly more than villages. Second word is 'Kanaal' – which means, mostly, a ditch. Stadskanaal, Musselkanaal. 'Veen' means turf: the boggy peaty moorland that was cut for fuel in the depression days, before the oil pipelines and the natural gas. The canals drain it – a network of tiny waterways. There are a great many; this country takes a lot of draining. But there is no watershed, and green scummy water dribbles vaguely in all directions – towards the Ems estuary, and down south towards rivers. The biggest of these canals have some mercantile use, and there is quite a lot of plodding barge traffic even now.

The funny thing is that the country is on the verge of a big upheaval. They found a 'bubble' of natural gas up here. To see what is about to happen one need only look at Lacq, in France – and this bubble is ten times the size of Lacq's. Traditionally, though, it has always been a very poor and barren land. Very little use for agriculture, and none at all for anything else. Penniless. But the government has already altered all that.

Railways and roads; factories processing milk, scrap

17

metal, paper. Big trucks with trailers boomed along broad autoways; new diesel railcars linked Groningen and Winschoten at one end of the province with Emmen and Coevorden at the other; there was a branch line to Assen, with connexions to the main line south.

More sophisticated industry had been tempted into following. A small but enterprising firm built coach and even aircraft bodies; another directed by a brilliant engineer, was internationally known for electronic equipment – 'second Philips' was the local boast. A daughter-firm of a huge combine was making wire and cable; and another, forty-five per cent of the total Dutch output of heat-resisting glassware.

The sleepy little place hardly knew itself now. For untold generations it had looked like an ingrowing toenail, with much the same way of thinking.

Tiny shops, dark and smelly – corsets and cough mixture; wooden shoes and flat caps of gaudy cheap tweed; weed-killer and sheepdip; lumps of wet salt pork and margarine – all airy and glassy now, with black and chromium fronts. Outside tumbledown farms with sagging thatched roofs now stood tinny, brightly-painted, brand-new autos. Behind soared concrete cowsheds and haybarns, and fire-engine-colour tractors hauled the swedes and the sugar beets in increasing masses at greater speeds towards ever greedier consumers.

Smelly canal backwaters, scummy green or inky black, were filled in, and the worn-out wood of collapsing wharves cleared up. Concrete came pouring out of huge striped urns that revolved everywhere like merry-go-rounds; bright pink brick streets ate up the rutted cart-tracks. The work-house-ward schools were gone and there was an annexe to the hospital and even a swimming bath. True, the county insane asylum still stood gaunt in the sour fields; the prunus and flowering-cherry trees were tiny and the grass verges sickly; the few old stunted oaks looked sad and lonely despite cheerful additions with golden cypress and Montana pine.

But the bustle of the burgomaster – and generous state funds – had infected the whole withered place with new seeds and spores. Rebirth.

The local people, and with them a swelling tide of strangers from congested metropolitan Holland, took with enthusiasm to easy work in sunny, canteen-and-canned-music factories. Pleasant change from trying to dig a living out of wet, black, stinking ground. Population had doubled and redoubled in ten years, and now blocks of flats and streets of tiny balconied brick houses – very Dutch, with extraordinarily large windows – surrounded and hid the surviving nineteenth-century cottages. But a few were still lived in, tiny, sad, depressing; witness still to the meanness, the bitterness and the pathos of life here for over a thousand years.

I saw quite a lot of this the first visit. Not the hour with the burgomaster – I spent the day strolling. Coffee in one café, a beer in another, and a greasy pork-chop lunch in the town's biggest, between a billiardtable and six commercial travellers, all with green Opel station wagons stuffed with samples and catalogues, all bolting their filthy chops with enthusiastic expense-account appetites.

It was wonderful winter weather, that first day. Windless, bright sun, and the canals frozen. The children stormed out whooping at four, and there instantly was the classic Dutch painting: a sun sinking redly behind the stepped gable and tiny spire of the Netherlands Reformed Church, and a thousand four-year-olds buttoned up to the eyes shrieking and tumbling on the old-fashioned, long wooden skates. My eyes were all on the houses, where the oblique beam of sun streamed in through a thousand enormous over-polished windows and lit up the interiors.

They looked like all the other Dutch interiors. Here a lumpy old coal stove, polished brilliant black, and 'gothic' wooden furniture upholstered in olive-green plush. There the streamlined grey oilburner, and 'contemporary' mushrooms of chairs with knitting-needle legs and pink or mauve 'moquette'. Either the old walnut veneer dresser, with a tiny diamond-pane window showing souvenir German wine glasses (bulbous green, with Loreleis painted on them) and turned chess-queen legs, or the flat slab of imitation teak. All proudly oiled and spotlessly dusted. Everywhere, of course, crammed with climbing plants, far too many lamps and at least three too many tables. Since Pieter de Hooch, Dutch interiors have gone downhill.

None of this told me much about the people who lived there. Were they too just like the ones in metroland? Had a thousand years in the 'Veen' ground produced a local type? There were local names – I saw several 'Van Veen' and 'Van der Veen' nameplates on doors.

I found a local weekly paper to take home, and seized on it with joy. And once at home again, I nearly wore it out. The cheap grey newsprint with its smudgy blunt press frayed at the folds and then disintegrated under the well-known heavy police hand and burning police eye of our brilliant officer. It told me a lot. Just for a start, births, deaths and marriages. And a real invention of 'the little province' – a careful column telling one who has arrived in our midst, with full details. Address he's come to, and come from. His name and his profession. All compiled from the careful indexing and filing of our industriously nosy functionaries in that damned town hall.

Here, in these columns, one could recognize the local people easily. If Piet Jansen the bricklayer from Zaandam had settled in the Dahlia Street, and Ria Bakker the secretary from Maassluis was now filling the Widow Pump's back room in the Vondel Street, it was doubtless fascinating to the locals, but not to me. Luckily, one could always tell.

The locals had ludicrous names. Ook and Goop and Unk.

Surnames as bad, and clans of course – generations of inter-marriage no doubt.

'Cold Comfort Farm,' said Arlette amusedly. 'Seth and Reuben, Dooms and Starkadders. No doubt there'll be sukebind and watervoles.'

Quite right; no exaggeration whatever.

'And a lot of heavy-handed rural fornication in summer. Rose Bernd all over again.'

I wasn't quite so sure about that one. The list of Sunday services in the paper was formidable. I counted carefully; there were seventeen different kinds of churches.

Obvious ones first, of course. Netherlands Renewed Protestants. Even more – Netherlands Reformed. A march of well-known 'chapel' sects: Baptists and Methodists, Unitarians and Congregationalists. The rather queer ones, not quite certain of acceptance outside a well-tried little clique – Jehovah's Witnesses, Christian Scientists, Roman Catholics (oh yes, definitely queer, here).

But what was one to say to the wilder Irvingite and Campbellite aberrations that flourished here in holy righteousness? Remonstrant Early Lutherans, Purged Presbyterians, Rigid Plymouth Brethren? Sects that didn't have churches – churches were neither rigid enough, nor purged enough. They had Meeting Places of God's Elect. All that was lacking was Aimée Semple McPherson. It was a list to make Elmer Gantry lick his lips in holy joy and clap his great pious meaty hands together and uplift his voice in vociferous sanctity.

'No Jews or Quakers,' remarked Arlette with interest.

'Plenty of by-Our-Lady horny-handed early Christians though – very early. Deacon Urk, Gravedigger Bloop, and Sexton Moogie, gathered round Dominie Prophecies-of-Malachi Thunk; she-that-commits-it-shall-be-cut-off.'

'Have a look,' said Arlette. 'Klaas Kip married Wilhel-mina Dina Regina Vos.'

'You've seen nothing yet – you haven't read the report of

the monthly meeting and tea-drinking of the Christian Rural Women. Carrie Nation presided at the bunfight. Takes one back a hundred years. Small towns in Iowa and South Dakota were like this in Elmer Gantry's extreme youth.'

The happenings in this remote, comic place, where a sham modernism hid but did not alter knotted, rooted survivals, were as ludicrous as the names. ·

I was reminded of two things when I first read the dossier and they never quite left me throughout the time I was there.

First was easy, an obvious one: the Staphorst affair. The international press had picked it up as an example of primitive survivals in a modern world. Staphorst is a village in Drente too, albeit the other end of the province. It has a closed little community and a sort of rural Calvinism un-equalled for hellfire savagery. They go to church in procession on Sundays, with downcast eyes and clasped Bibles, and the men have been known to break the cameras of gawping tourists. A pair here had been caught in adultery, had been – by report – among other things drawn through the village in a cart and pelted with tomatoes or something.

The other memory was of a French film based on the classic case of the 'Witches of Salem'. Reading the dossier, I had thought that twentieth-century Zwinderen had a good deal in common with seventeenth-century Massachusetts. Not only the pillory and the stocks, but the stake and the noose were not very far away here.

Not so very much had happened, factually, and yet one could understand why the Procureur-Général in Leeuwarden, and his colleague in Amsterdam, had taken this so seriously. Two women had committed suicide, and a third had had to be led gently away by men in white coats. There had been an outbreak of anonymous letters – a blackmailing poison-pen – and nobody knew quite how many of these had not come to light.

That was not so very much. But there was more, intangible but perceptible. Like Salem, the whole place sounded hysterical, neurotic. Neighbourhood squabbles tended to be started by virtuous housewives, shrilly accusing other virtuous housewives of immorality. There were too many, and they were too much alike.

There was a lot of immorality – a bit too much. I had the file on the past year's police court cases behind-locked-doors. Incest, mm; never quite unknown in these ingrown inter-married districts. But rather too much rape, indecent exposure, dissemination of pornography, obscene dancing in cafés, underhand prostitution – underneath all the drum-beating and bell-ringing on Sundays, there was a sort of sexy itch. One could not get at it properly. Not only were the reports in a language so stilted, so proper and so bureaucratic that I could hardly understand them myself, practised as I am, but the witnesses were excessively hang-dog and evasive, not to speak of wholesale perjury, obvious if quite unprovable.

One knows what 'he then attempted to commit an offence' means, but one cannot cross-examine a nine-year-old girl in court, after a respectable fifty-eight-year-old farmer had been caught by his wife pulling her pants off in a hayloft. He said things. What? Child couldn't say and wife wouldn't.

This letter writing. Something was common knowledge, more had been debated, in secret but subject to leakage. Some was dead secret – they said.

Neither the municipal police – always stilted in language – nor the State Recherche – unembarrassed, flowery, practised, but empty – were much help. There were facts, but so scarce and vague, and by now so thumbed and hammered, as to be unrecognizable. And this letter-writing was undiminished, but how much was there? How long had it been going on? How many letters were burned, thrown down the lavatory? And how many were kept, re-read, pored over? Even

23

enjoyed? The whole thing had been frightened underground by three-times-repeated banging and poking by heavy-handed police.

What facts there were were boring. For instance, the letters were composed in the classic way of letters and words clipped from the local paper – the one I had bought. Helpful! But nobody seemed to have thought much about the style, though it interested me. The language was quite practised, that of somebody, one would say, accustomed to putting words on paper. Yet it was stiff and cramped – not a normal feature of personal letters. Not an unschooled person: no spelling mistakes, and carefully accurate punctuation – too careful; it was painful. The letters were formal, selfconscious, grammatically careful but with no eye for a simple everyday word. The style of someone who thinks that a television announcer is the perfect model.

There was no real obscenity, either, in the verbal sense. A dirty-minded bourgeois. The majority of the letters that had been found were to women, but some were to men. Hm, youngish married women. Were they simply quicker to bring such things into the open? Apart from the three 'victims' there was little known about these women. They were not suspected of anything.

This chasing after suspects is always a bore. I am always more interested in victims. I was now.

A fat lot of good it had done here looking for suspects. That part of the inquiry had been to my mind the most thoroughly botched up. They had found one really juicy, promising suspect, and had ended up with a fist full of gravel. They'd gone on the classical supposition that some-one who writes sexy letters to women is most likely to be an elderly bachelor. When they found, on the doorstep, an elderly bachelor, with eccentric habits, a peculiar past, and a secretive nature, they stuck to him with a stupid obstinacy ... Mark, he was certainly interesting.

The idea of a woman writer had never been taken

seriously. Yes, perhaps poison-pen letters are traditionally an elderly spinster's work, but all the elderly spinsters around there seemed irreproachable. And though there was jealousy in the letters, it was directed at the men, not at the women. A lesbian in Drente? Pooh pooh.

There had been a hunt for psychopaths of course, and anyone who had ever been caught in a moral scandal, however slight. The State Recherche – very very thorough indeed – had even unearthed the fact that the burgomaster, earlier in his career, had once been thought rather too fond of sitting little girls on his lap. Charming; Burgomaster Humbert N. Pctit of Larousse, Ill. But nothing had ever been seriously proved, and there was certainly no evidence, not a scrap, to link him with any of this.

After motive, they had, with relish, attacked opportunity. They had reached vast numbers of conclusions, and nothing whatever proved one way or the other.

I let out a sort of moan. This might all be intensely funny, but I wasn't at all sure I was greatly amused.

Arlette was busily packing her precious gramophone records.

# 6

The first working days in Zwinderen were spent observing the manners and customs of Drente; Van der Valk feeling like an anthropologist among the Papuans. Ethnological studies indeed. I felt a bit like the schoolboy who wrote on his examination paper, 'Customs beastly ... manners none', and left it at that.

But I had a suitcase filled with books, newspaper clippings, and perfectly genuine files from the Ministry of the Interior, which I was agreeably surprised to find passionately interesting.

What, in Zwinderen, did they buy, wear, eat, drink, approve of? It wasn't right from the start, at all, what Arlette bought, wore, ate, drank or approved of. For information about all sorts of eccentric things, often simply because I had noticed something and been puzzled, I went to the burgomaster's secretary; she was the greatest help. She knew everybody and everything; seemed to be never at a loss, and was quite willing to instruct a responsible functionary; perhaps it flattered her sense of importance. It needed no flattering; she was important. Of course as confidential secretary she had access to all but the most important decisions, and that meant virtually everything that concerned the little town. She knew, too, all the local politics.

From her I learned of the long-standing quarrel between the Head of Parks and Gardens and the Municipal Gas Works. She knew the whole history of the throat-cutting between the contractors for the new Garden Suburb, and the figures of the loss taken by the subcontractor in electrical equipment for the sake of prestige – it had been she who had seen that he had tried to make the loss up by skimping the workmanship. She was illuminating about the solitary Communist member of the council, about the row over the new hospital equipment that all the doctors claimed was inadequate, about too much having been spent on the swimming bath, and got back by cheese-paring on the new dustbin lorries. She seemed to wave a sceptre over everybody. The burgomaster swore by her tact and ability – Miss Burger could always get it done. I found her myself a pleasant woman – no great beauty, but nice brown eyes and attractive feuille-morte hair – shiny, healthy-looking – and a good clear skin.

Arlette was tedious; bombarding everything with sarcasms. The Mimosastraat, to begin with.

'Why Mimosa? And why is there a Mimosa Street in every piddling town in Holland? None of these people have

26

ever seen mimosa in their lives. Dahlias, tulips, narcissi – I find that understandable . . .'

Dear Arlette. She comes from the department of the Var and thinks that all the mimosa in the world is her own personal property.

Curses were heaped upon the anthracite stove, though it was modern; upon the curtains in the bedroom, which did, it was true, have an aggressively rural flower-pattern; upon the 'three-piece suite', a bargain, shop-soiled after being used for a Show House by a local emporium; upon the extraordinary shower in the bathroom. I admitted her right to that; one was supposed to sit, apparently, in a kind of pit at waist-level – a masterpiece of plumbing that would rouse an incredulous guffaw even at the sources of the Amazon.

By the third day she was settling in; moving furniture with zest, as though determined to leave her individual stamp on even this borrowed anonymous shoe-box of a house. But she was still acid at meals.

'Milk here's undrinkable.'

Aha, it was one of my items of knowledge, which I brought out of my rag-bag of Drentse lore. 'Seems they like it like that. Call it High-Pasteurized.'

'Which to me means scorched. Butter – rendered cow-hide. And the butchers! People live here, I think, on fat salt pork and mince.'

Mince is nearly the dirtiest word in Arlette's vocabulary.

'But what I find worst of all is the way they stare. Stare, stare, blatantly, openly, uncaring. Stand there transfixed, with great dull eyes, gaping.'

It was true. Even at me – one would say a harmless-look-ing object. Here an Amsterdammer, it seemed, was an Indian from the Peruvian uplands, plus blanket and llama. The peasants did stare consumedly; little girls poked at each other and dissolved in giggles. Poor Arlette, with her accent that becomes strong in shops, and she still says 'in a box' when she means tinned. And her hair in a fringe, with a beret on top ... The women here wore scarves over hair like an O-Cedar mop, and the 'ladies' wonderful hairy hats. They asked for a pound of mince, and took obediently what they were given. I felt a little sorry for the butcher. Arlette's butcher has been accustomed for years to her poking, coming behind the counter, even pursuing the poor fellow into his own cold-room. He is used by now to 'Too fresh again', and keeps her steak a week longer than anyone else's ...

'Be discreet,' I told her. 'Disguise yourself. Still, I trundle about all day in a grey suit, clutching a brief-case of crudely imitated pigskin, and even I am stared at. They look, and guess immediately that your name is neither Unk nor Flook and that you don't belong to the clan.'

'I am discreet. I shall burst myself with discretion. I found Beaujolais, so-called, but in Albert Heijn, so it might well be drinkable. Dear Albert, his shop is a home from home to me.'

Leek soup for supper, and chicory salad – not a very Drente meal, despite the presence of undoubtedly Drente butter. I settled down for a good go at the letters. Arlette had been much reconciled by discovering that here one could get German television; I had hired a set for her that morning and she was busy with the new toy. The letters were very boring; I found myself staring entranced at the delightful hair-styles of the German announcer-girls. But we must be resolute.

The longest file was the first suicide. She had been the wife, poor girl, of the technical director – second in command – of the little electronics factory; the man who, with the owner, made up the inventive team. What did we know about him, first? Reinders, Will, forty-three. Came from Dordrecht. Impressive engineering qualifications: evidently a brilliant chap. Religion Reformed. Well regarded in his profession. Locally spoken of as calm and steady. Mixes very little with Zwinderen notables, but said to be friendly and easy to get on with. Very dedicated, takes profession very seriously; certainly coming man. Alone or with the boss (who lives in Baarn but comes up at least twice a week) makes frequent trips all over Holland and abroad. Point is that wife was often alone. Absolutely no police record – what a blameless individual!

Wife's name Betty; thirty-six, born in Groningen, religion Reformed, first marriage. No children. Church-goer, whereas husband was not, but thought of as a little flighty, even frivolous. Active however in various do-good social activities. There had been a rumour that she had got too friendly with a young draughtsman at the factory, who had as a consequence been sacked. But this had not been taken very seriously, since the letters did not threaten her with any such thing as a scandal. It was the husband that was threatened. He was, according to the writer, a dirty dog, and the implication was that the writer would make the girl a much more satisfactory lover. Mm.

They had been found in her jewellery box after her death – not the first to come to light, but the first series. Was it a series? There was no way of telling. Undated, and no way of fixing even chronological order. Moreover there had been phone calls, and after the first contact there were few letters – if they were, indeed, all here.

Naturally, every possible indication had been followed up. Nothing for me there. Just that hint in the style that appeared to have struck nobody much.

'You may be of opinion . . . I am well aware with what he is occupied . . . your position of standing . . . wallow in corruption and hypocrisy . . . was that not an agreeable surprise?' A sort of old-fashioned commercialese. All the letters had the same tone – a kind of affectionate menace. Offers of 'rescue' and 'protection'. Frequent references to the Eye of God and the Ear of God – both, apparently, the writer. The later letters were lyrical about the joys of being in bed together, but nothing showed definitely whether these joys were anticipatory or reminiscent.

Police had raced to the director of the lunatic asylum for a psychiatric opinion. He had read the letters, shrugged, and said, reasonably, that the writer might well be insane but he had no opinion to offer on the basis of these letters alone. Handwriting would have given more and sharper indications, but . . . 'I have no judgements beyond those of any normal detached person, without more to go on.'

Quite. The letters were mildly dotty, in much the same way as the letters of a fanatic about racing pigeons or model aeroplanes. It was no more and no less to my mind than the frustrated gentlemen who make indecent propositions to telephone-service girls. Even the explicit remarks could be total fantasy.

One letter had a different tone. It was in the dossier, but there was no proof that the writer was the same. It might have been someone who had a letter, and decided to take a leaf out of the book. It was to a young girl of sixteen – there had been an earlier letter which she had destroyed, terrified. Reconstructed it read, more or less. 'You little fool. I saw you. Unless you do what I tell you, everything will be known. Show this to no one, but watch carefully for the next, and do exactly what I tell you.'

The one they had read: 'Cross the bridge tonight at nine exactly. You will get instructions at the right moment. Wear your beige coat, but under it you are not to wear any clothes at all.'

It had gone too far. Shocked even more than frightened, the girl had done nothing, but had finally gone to Mum. Who had had the sense to go straight to the police. Too late, and there had been no more letters. It was one of the first that had come to light, and had remained disconnected.

That looked simply like the work of some elderly voyeur. Possibly.

There was only one other series anything like complete: the unfortunate woman who had gone round the bend. She sat all day in apathy; there was nothing to be got out of her. She had been the wife of a Protestant minister, and quite a mild, reasonable one at that; not one of the hellfire sects. A man against whom there had never been a breath of scandal. This was a puzzle. The letters were all full of religion. But if, say, Reinders was attacked for being an enemy of religion – which seemed the tone often – why attack a man known to all as deeply devout? The unhappy man had renounced his living and vanished into obscurity. Police had questioned him, but had nothing to hold him for. He had upheld vehemently that there was no truth in any of the suggestions.

He was one of the few men to have had letters.

'Do you think that nobody knows about the book of photographs in the locked bookcase? Your wife would be interested. Perhaps I will tell everybody. You would get an enthusiastic reception on Sunday then.' He had not told the wife. He had done nothing. He had not understood why his wife should have acted strangely. He had disregarded the letter as a ridiculous untruth from someone evidently insane.

Why keep it?

To show the police in case there were more.

Had it never occurred to him that his wife might also have had letters?

No, it hadn't, unhappily.

Had he been afraid to draw attention to the suggestion? Was it true?

The wife's were much the same as Betty's. 'If you do not want the scandal to ring through the whole country, you must follow the instructions you will receive implicitly.'

Had she? Had anything happened? Was it all just wish-fulfilment?

The other suicide – wife of the manager of the milk-products business – had left no letters. It was only an assumption that she had had any.

I rather thought she had. The husband had acted rather queerly, to my mind.

Police actions had been based on mutual acquaintance. What persons had been in contact with all these others? Remarkably many. None of them remotely suggestive. Whose telephone to tap, whose house to watch? Every idea had petered out.

The whole affair had been kept from the public – but a lot was certainly known. And the public reacted. That large number of respectable wives who had got tetchy with each other in public. That quite violently heated audience for a rather scruffy café where on two occasions – meaning two had been proved – a woman had done a decidedly daring strip-tease. Who knew what went on in a small town? Everything was known, and nothing.

Everything could be seen. The Dutch, especially the more provincial Dutch, do not draw their curtains even at night. There are many explanations of this; I have always thought it due to anxiety – the Dutch neurosis. The anxiety lest anyone thinks us not normal, not conforming, not 'respectable'.

'We have nothing to hide,' announce those curtains.

Hadn't they? Nothing?

There is a favourite Dutch pastime that they call 'shadow-watching'. Everybody in Zwinderen does it, I have noticed already. As the name implies, it is an evening occupation, towards twilight. You sit by your own open curtains, one lamp in your room lit, and you observe.

Every home has huge windows, front and back. Walls are paper thin. There is almost nothing one can do that is not seen and heard instantly – and as for flats . . . This could be called a typical small-town provincial crime. And given a mildly deranged person, two a penny anywhere, you arrived with unpleasant ease at multiple death. Which, however provincial, is as frightening, as horrid, as difficult to stop, as worrying to authority, as the classic psychopath multiple murderer of cities – Jack the Ripper, Franz Becker, and all the other textbook cases. What was the difference between knifing a prostitute, strangling a child, and badgering a housewife into insanity or suicide?

People died, didn't they?

Resolutely, I shut the file, with its thick supplement of police conclusions. These were really pretty inept. I reach inept conclusions too, but I try not to let other people read them. There is the written report that is intelligent, and there is the written report that at least sounds intelligent.

Example of ineptitude: a reference in one letter to 'eleven tomorrow'. An annotation put the illuminating query, 'Is this a Saturday?' Meaning that if the writer was an employed person, Saturday would be his only free morning.

Ve-r-y helpful.

Further down they had all worked on the assumption that since most of these people were roughly classifiable as bourgeoisie, the writer would be either self-employed, or in a position to find free time at any moment of the day if he wished. Not only inept: asinine. But incidentally it had helped to thicken the blanketing haze of suspicion round the one promising suspect: a certain Mr Besançon. I reached for the file on Mr Besançon. Arlette, who has the un-Dutch idea that tea at night is bad for one, had made two glasses of fresh lemonade with the peel in it, and honey.

'Honey, honey?' She thinks this funny. Funny, honey. There was a lot of very attractive steam. I fished out my lemon-peel and chewed on it in a greedy way.

# 7

It began with an elaborate summary. Points indicating or supporting suspicion. And, to be fair of course, points in favour. Which were, briefly, that no ground existed beyond stupid prejudice to suspect the man of anything at all.

Followed a pretty complete picture of his present circumstances, and a long row of dockets – all that was known of his extraordinary chequered past. I read the whole thing, absorbed. Very, very interesting indeed. Man was in his sixties. Lives alone. Widower.

A stranger, a Jew, an intellectual.

Known to be nervously deranged; result of wartime experiences.

Lives in house with high wall – practically the only one in Holland. You can't see what he does all day.

Works at home, in own time, in own way, at own pleasure.

Known to take long solitary walks at night. Has also been seen at six in the morning.

Is courteous, formal, but shy and distant in relations with everybody.

Seems to shun human contact.

Has telephone. Does regular work for electronics firm. Has contact with husband of dead woman number one.

Is known as inventor of mysterious apparatus and devices.

Speaks Dutch in formal, correct but slightly stilted way.

Speaks German perfectly; French well; Russian well.

Suspected pacifist, suspected pro-Russian. Lukewarm on alliances, patriotism. Low on political consciousness.

Practises no religion. Never been known to profess any, either Jewish or any other.

Professes, on the contrary, fear of newspapers, radios, television, parties, associations, committees, organizations (everything, in short, that makes Dutch life so agreeable).

There were some perfectly charming annotations here too. 'Having no newspapers in the house, access to newsprint – i.e., to cut out letters – presumed limited.'

Of course, the greengrocer does have that habit of wrapping cabbages in old newspapers. Arlette starts reading them instead of getting on with the cabbage.

There is a housekeeper, a middle-aged woman who looks after Mr Besançon out of charity and refuses a wage. She says indignantly that any connexion with revolting happenings is quite unthinkable.

During protracted interviews with many most experienced police-officers, Monsieur Besançon showed irritation, nervous strain, and agitation in moments of fatigue. All kept within bounds, all balanced by politeness, self-control, patience and understanding of officers' unpleasant duties. All this is explainable by his past life – which includes interrogation by the Gestapo, years in camps, and forced labour. All the policemen agreed on this.

One last thing struck me – and hard, because it was the one thing I would have given real weight to. An irrational feeling. It was the final annotation, by the State Recherche officer.

'I have been many times struck in course of conversation with Mr Besançon by the conviction that he possessed some secret. This led me to a persistent belief that he was the author of the crimes under investigation, but that conclusive evidence, since he is certainly a very clever man, would be hard to find. After two days, however, of rigorous interrogation, I am bound to state that this feeling rests upon no factual basis and must therefore be disregarded.'

That, I thought, is damned funny language from the State Recherche. The feeling he had was so strong that he felt he had to put it in the report. But no-factual-basis, so he feels impelled to warn any reader of said report not to give way to unsupported suspicion. (The police had, quite handsomely, apologized for giving Besançon several thoroughly disagreeable weeks. He had answered politely that he had quite understood.)

The conclusion is typical. Since there is nothing tangible, the theory must be suppressed. Quite right; I have got into trouble often because of these little men that tell me things, who live in my stomach. Remember Edward G. Robinson, in that wonderful part in *Double Indemnity*? He was right. I have been right too, sometimes.

Sometimes I haven't been right.

Anyway, I'm not going to get feelings just because a constipated security officer tells me not to. If I did, it would probably be because he had told me not to, with his damned cheek.

But I am certainly going to try and get to know Mr Besançon. Not because I suspect him of anything. He just sounds an interesting man, and everybody else here sounds, I am bound to state, if I may be allowed to quote the State Recherche's fancy language, remarkably dull. I went back to the dossier.

Born, it began, in 1901, of a South-German Jewish family that had removed itself over the centuries from Prague to München to Breda, in Dutch Brabant. Family were watchmakers there for the last three generations.

Apprenticed in family business, and early showed remarkable aptitude. As an adult, gained a rapidly increasing reputation for making unusual timepieces, including so-called eternal clocks. Sun, wind, waterpowered. Progressed to speciality in ingenious time-switch mechanisms.

Had a strong amateur interest in astronomy, and built telescopes as a pastime. Formed, through all this, a connexion with the firm of Carl Zeiss. Went, during the thirties, frequently to Jena, where he collaborated to some extent in the early experiments on planetariums, the artificial heavens driven by clockwork mechanisms.

Was, however, in Breda at the time of Hitler's invasion of Holland, and was promptly arrested with entire family. He then disappeared. Was saved from extermination – suffered by entire family down to most distant connexions – by obscure agency. Possibly the firm of Zeiss signalled that his skills were worth more to the Reich than two gold teeth.

He was, in any case, forced to work on various secret weapon projects, but was never, he recalled wryly, left on any one scheme long enough either to do it any good or any harm. He passed from mines to rocketry, and with another of those sudden whimsical decisions common during that epoch was suddenly detached from the whole thing and brought to Berlin. Someone, he hazarded, knew that he spoke Russian – but there were others who did too ... he wasn't complaining. During the big Russian advance of '44, he was used constantly by Intelligence (Schellenberg) but was drawn more and more into the Kaltenbrünner-Müller orbit. His work, officially, was to penetrate Russian Intelligence reports, working on codes and communications, but he realized later that he had been used in the incredibly involved system of double agents directed by Müller.

He was, in fact, being used as one of the key figures in secret correspondence with the Russians, but was never allowed to see enough of the complete picture to shed any real light, or give conclusive evidence.

In the final days of the Berlin siege he was held prisoner in the Bunker, still in almost daily contact with Bormann, and as the Russians entered the city was shot and left for dead by a member of the Bormann entourage. He was discovered by the Russians, patched up roughly in a military hospital, held prisoner for many months – then suddenly, inexplicably released; a typical Russian performance.

They had come to the conclusion, presumably, after interrogating him, that the man would never be any good any more. He did not know enough to be a valuable counter-espionage prize, and as inventor, even as technical craftsman – finished. Physically, indeed, he recovered from his head wound, but not only did he develop a nervous disease, he had also a mental block. The disease was a kind of slow degeneration of the central nervous system, something similar to Parkinson's disease. He could walk upright, but he had the constant trembling, and his vision was affected. He could no longer mend an alarm clock, let alone handle fine machinery. And the mental block was not so much, perhaps, the loss of inventive capacity as of the will to do anything, to see what made it tick. He had holes in his memory; a kind of disassociation. He looked at simple mechanical contrivances and could not even remember their names or function.

He had spent, inevitably, years more in observation clinics, resettlement camps, an atom of flotsam like many more, difficult to help, wearisome and unco-operative; a nuisance, a worry, a responsibility. He was no use to anybody any more. He had the arrogance and obstinacy of the outcast. Refused to give evidence against war-criminals. What was the use, he said. Would God not know the sheep from the goats? Would hanging all the Germans take away Treblinka or Baby Yar? And what could he tell them they did not by now know? He would have nothing to do with other Jews. He said he wished he had been exterminated too – what was left of life? No family, no job, no skill, no friends, nothing.

In the end he had drifted back to Holland. Not to Breda, but wandering about vaguely, a burden on charitable organizations that were sorry for him, but glad to get rid of him. Finally he had turned up in Drente. He liked it here, he said; there were no Jews, nor Christians either (a remark received charitably, like many more).

In Zwinderen it had been the burgomaster, new then but as energetic as now, who had found a way out of the impasse, with patience and intelligence. He had seen that nothing was any use without some scrap of independence. He had got a pension for the man, and a disability grant, and a compensation from Germany. And a roof. Besançon had been delighted by the burgomaster's offer of a little cottage that belonged to the lunatic asylum, tucked in a corner of the grounds there, damp and primitive, used in the nineteenth century to house some turnkey. Nobody in Holland wanted that: he did. He liked the high stone wall, the gloomy cypresses and yews. He dug in the tiny sunless garden with his first show of enthusiasm. Rehabilitation had begun.

He went, a little later, to the burgomaster, offering to do any work he was still capable of. That was tactfully refused, but the offer was passed to the first factories then being established in Drente. Here he picked up a connexion: the electronics firm could use, they said, a Russian translator from time to time. This spread, and now there were half a dozen firms sending him scientific reports for translation. He had learned pharmaceutical and chemical symbols – or relearned them, along with his lost mathematics – and was much appreciated by his employers. Nobody, they said warmly, could translate Russian or technical German with such lucidity. Nobody was so good at seizing relevant extracts, making a clear and brief paraphrase, piercing the jungle of administrative or bureaucratic phrase, marshalling the kernel of facts in a long waffling report that might cover three years' work of some dedicated but vague scientific person somewhere behind the Urals.

His writing was too shaky to be usable, but the grateful electronics firm designed and built a special typewriter for him; it was the owner, too, that found him a housekeeper.

Now, he said, he was happy. He worked, he earned. He bought books and records. He took long walks and tended his garden. Occasionally someone from 'his' firms came to consult him on some point; he saw nobody else. He had been invited to people's houses; he came courteously and behaved perfectly, but let it be understood that he preferred not to come. People had learned to respect his small eccentricities.

Of course, when he appeared in the village, as he sometimes did for gum or string, carbon paper or a pair of socks, children whooped and people whispered. He was used by the peasantry as a bogy-man; many a tiny Drentse cropped-head was threatened with 'the Russian professor'. But his manner, indifferent, formal, always courteous, conquered even peasant suspicions. When he raised his hat so politely to some dumpy mottled milkmaid behind the pencils and envelopes, pointing with a shaky forefinger at a roll of scotch tape, he could hardly be thought of as a bogy.

He had been here ten years now. He had got shakier, his eyesight worse. He could still walk upright, but uncertainly, with a stick. But mentally he had not failed.

He wore corduroy trousers like the workmen; cheap ready-made coats; he had a 'good suit', indistinguishable from that of a local churchwarden. He had experimented with hats, and wore at present an extraordinary green thing, Dutch-Tyrolean, cut from hairy cardboard. He sometimes shuffled out in the wooden shoes he used for gardening.

Nothing about him, though, of the comic-strip absent-minded scientist. His hair was cut short and he used a clothes-brush vigorously. At sixty he was trim, neat, and tidy; a small thin man with authority still in his carriage. He had fine flowers behind his high grey wall, and on the sunny side a cherry tree facing the little window of his living-room. The little cottage was only two rooms, with a sort of lean-to kitchen at the back, and a septic-tank lavatory across a tiny yard. He had electricity but no gas.

He always wore dark glasses over his sharp blue eyes. The doctor had given him maybe another five years. These nervous degeneration diseases are deadly, but extremely slow. He hoped, he said, to have another two of useful work.

He had been examined dozens of times by every conceivable sort of neurologist and psychiatrist. Perfectly sane, perfectly lucid. Remarkably well adjusted to severe trauma.

Might such a person write threatening obscene letters to respectable married women; creep about peering and listening for some little human misdeed or indiscretion?

Even if he might he hadn't known any of them, or anything about them. But a theory had been built up by some artful imbecile of a policeman. The electronics firm manufactured, among other specialized gadgets, tiny microphones and listening sets of incredible power and sensitivity. One of their recent efforts could (classified, highly sccrct, but the policeman had wormed out certain facts) pick up conversational tones at twenty metres or more, through the walls of houses. Even disregarding the legend that former-engineer Besançon was a conjuring-trick king, had he ever, through his work, had access to any such thing? It had been investigated; answer definitely negative. He had never even been in the factory. Still, it was a seductive notion. How else had the letter-writer found out some of the things he appeared to know?

'Time to go to bed,' said Arlette, yawning. 'There's been quite good variety from München. My German's getting better, but that Bayerische dialect is beyond me. Come on, get unglued.'

Part two: 'Acquaintance'

# 1

Having read that exhaustive dossier, and being quite convinced that this man had nothing whatever to do with writing naughty letters, it was, I admit, a pure waste of time to go and see him. Quite unjustifiable. But I was enjoying the sensation of doing unjustifiable things – there was nobody shouting at me to justify myself. It was not just vulgar curiosity that took me in his direction next day: I had to see for myself – and was it perhaps the expectation, too, of finding somebody human at last in this spot? I thought that my alias would be enough to get me into this little fortress behind the wall of the lunatic asylum. What then? I had no idea.

It was at the point just outside the town where the bog had been halted. Pavements petered out, street-lighting stopped abruptly, and the muddy digging of foundations for new houses gave way to sodden fields and sparse, tormented trees, with uninviting drainage ditches every hundred metres. A gate in the high wall had an admonishing notice about Unauthorized Persons; I peered in.

Nothing exciting; fields. Evidence that the lunatic asylum had cows, grew its own vegetables, and kept its own chickens. A roadway led to a ragged belt of poplars, behind which I could see bits of a vast dingy building. I went on along my road, reached after a minute a corner, and sure enough around the corner I found another gate, and could see evergreens over the walls. Gate was a rusty iron affair, backed with a sort of 'blindage' of galvanized metal that blocked the view between the bars. I greatly envied Mr

Besançon all this privacy. I found an old chain dangling among ivy tendrils, pulled, and heard a cowbell tinkle.

Woman in apron, sturdy, shapeless. Wore spectacles, apple-cheeked, straggly brown hair; Dutch woman like five million more. She approved of my taking my hat off and tendering one of the mumbo-jumbo cards.

'He's working, but if you'll come in I'm sure he'll . . . do you mind just waiting here?'

Yes; door opened straight into the living-room. I admired the flower-borders, though it was February and there was little to see. Even on the shadowed, drippy side of the garden, where thick brambly undergrowth was enough to cut off the view of the asylum altogether, there were rhododendrons and azaleas.

'Will you please come in?' She bustled off towards a nice smell of stew. I bowed, said good morning, and turned to shut the door. A thin neat man, in old trousers and a baggy jacket, had got up politely. One had a fleeting first impression of short grey hair, a face with very deep sunken wrinkles but a powerful energetic mouth and eyes that flashed still behind the dark glasses.

'Good morning.' Voice deep and resonant.

'My name is Van der Valk; I'm from the Ministry of the Interior; my field of study includes town-planning. There is no need to trouble you, but since I was passing . . .'

'But please sit down; allow me to take your hat.'

There were two shabby arm-chairs with a coffee-table between, and a standard lamp. Mr Besançon sat down again at his desk and examined his guest calmly. It was strange; I at once had the feeling that I was sitting in the wrong chair. As a policeman, it is my business to sit behind desks and look at people that way. The man was immediately impressive; he had a patient watchfulness. I launched into a gabble about possible demolition of the asylum, possible road-widening; blahblah.

'Am I scheduled for demolition?'

'That is too sweeping. In the event of such a decision, you would be notified well in advance; if you objected you would have every opportunity to put your case.'

Mild smile; faintly raised eyebrow. 'I am attached to this house, strangely.'

'Do not disquiet yourself; no decision has yet been made or will be made for quite a time. I really only came to sound your opinion.'

'My opinion is that I will not live very long. If these changes are postponed a year, I shall, I think, have very little to say. I am attacked, I must tell you, by a slow but mortal disease. But I should be happy if I were left in peace for what time I have left.'

'I think I can guarantee you some years without interruption.' I sincerely hoped that no municipal busybody really did have a road-widening project; it was perfectly possible.

Again the faint smile. 'More than enough . . . I suppose that you have informed yourself about my circumstances?'

'I have access to all information normally available to the Ministry,' sounding correctly prim. I thought I was doing this quite well.

'Just so.'

'Such details are necessarily incomplete.'

'So you make a point of calling on people who may live – let's say along a road scheduled for rebuilding.'

'When we can.'

'That is conscientious. And courteous. My experience of officials from Ministries is that they frequently have both qualities, but that their function seems to prevent the free exercise of either.'

My turn for the faint smile. Really, this fellow was shrewd.

'We do our best. It is painful to be criticized for what, to the uninformed eye, simply looks like turning defenceless people out of their homes.'

'Painful, but the state functionary grows an extra skin. Perhaps they have to. I am very grateful that you should spare the time to call on me.'

'We learn' – thinking I was being sly – 'to make time our servant. The wheels of Ministries are slow.'

'Ah,' reflective nod. 'You have plenty of time. Most functionaries bustle, always in a hurry. You have a bird's-eye view – in a manner of speaking – of people as well as sites, streets, ciphers, statistics. Most interesting.'

'Certainly.' I did not quite get the drift but admired the way he was cross-examining me – in a manner of speaking.

'Perhaps my experience has been too one-sided. It is the lower echelon, is it not, that adopts that bustling air, that fiction that there is never time for anything, that determination to obliterate the individual. The tiny self-importance of the village postmaster; once he has a rubber stamp in his hand he imagines that he embodies all the dignity of the State. Whereas you are plainly a senior official.'

'That is so.' I was being driven like a sheep, and interested enough not to care.

'Since you are not in a hurry,' inexorably, 'may I offer you a cup of coffee?'

'That would be kind.'

'I will ask Mrs Bakhuis – she generally brings me some. . .'

'I am tempted to think,' coming back with deliberate steps – the trembling was noticeable, but not disconcerting, 'that as a general rule policemen, perhaps, are fortunate among state servants, in having more obligatory contact with human beings. Even rather objectionable humans, who smell, who could do with delousing, are preferable to none.'

'And yet, if I am to believe what I hear, you are not very fond of the human race.'

'There have been times, you see, when I smelt and needed delousing. A thing quite inconceivable to a civil servant. The pressure upon functionaries to spend more and more time shut away in little cells, monastically devoted to their in and out trays – it is hardly fair on them.'

I felt like saying straight out what I had come for. What was the point of fencing further? This man was not guilty of any little, dotty, pathetic crimes. But I had to play the scene out a little.

'Aren't you tending towards special pleading? Every type of state servant has his particular problems. His questions of conscience, call it.'

He did not answer. He studied his guest with a placid look. I studied the surroundings. There were no pictures, but there were many home-made bookshelves. Lots of books, rows of cardboard files, doubtless containing his work, a shelf full of records. Tidy, for a man who lived alone. A shabby poverty, but not genteel, not ashamed. Those books were in all the major languages of Europe, and they all looked well handled.

Why were there no pictures? Did the man prefer things heard to things seen? . . . Mrs Thing came in with a pleasant smile and two cups of coffee. I have often wondered why the Dutch keep the coffee-pot in the kitchen, as though it were something to be ashamed of.

The door behind the housekeeper shut; we stirred the coffee. I offered him a cigarette, which he shook his head at slightly. I had a feeling we were coming to the point.

'Functionaries,' I said, 'good or bad, sensitive or not, one thing they all have in common is their professionalism. In the last analysis, they're getting paid for it.'

I had been expecting the reaction, but not that it would be so direct.

'Are you by any chance a policeman?'

To that kind of question, one cannot hesitate or shuffle. 'Yes.'

'I have been visited by so many, you see,' politely.

'That you penetrate me so easily shows that I can't be a new kind.'

'The first to be frank.'

'Perhaps I have started work with a different assumption. You don't fit my notions of this type of crime.'

'What type of crime?'

'You mean you don't know?'

'I have never been told,' simply, 'what it was that I was suspected of doing or being.'

'Oh dear. I suppose that's typical. You were suspected of being the author of anonymous blackmailing letters.'

I was watching closely; a very strange expression passed rapidly over the strong facial muscles. I could not quite put a name to it. Relief from apprehension?

'How stupid I am not to have guessed, after all the questioning.'

'I am surprised you didn't.' I was, too; the man was intelligent; more than that, he used his mind.

'I am an innocent fellow; it simply never occurred to me. Now, of course, I realize that I am an obvious suspect. Eccentric, probably mentally deranged, slightly sinister to village eyes – aha, now I see.'

'Why do you call yourself sinister?'

'In a village . . . A Jew, living behind a wall, avoiding people. I had understood that I would be suspect.'

'But it bothered you, to be suspected?'

'No, not really. Only peasant superstition.'

'Quite so. Yet you were worried.'

'Worried at the unceasing pressure of suspicion from officials. That is not superstition; it is, alas, a hard fact. Relays of policemen, always increasing in importance. The last were State Recherche. What would those gentlemen have to do with anonymous letters?'

'Two people have died – and the matter has still not been cleared up. The authorities have taken this seriously. It is vague; obscure.'

'I see. And you do not suspect me of anything still?'

I got up.

'I try never to suspect anybody of anything. I try to wait until I know.'

'I have grown over-sensitive.'

'I can see that. But will it worry you if I come back?'

'You do, then, suspect me of something.'

'No. I just like talking.'

'Come whenever you like. I am always here – but I am at a loss to see how that can profit you.'

'Everything profits me. And I like unusual people. They force one to think about things.' I picked up my hat. I could see well enough that he preferred to be left alone, but I knew that he would not show me hostility, now that he knew who I was. Using this man as a sparring partner would lighten my days, here in Zwinderen. Too bad if he didn't like it.


## 2


The Mimosa Street, where I now lived, is a street exactly like ten thousand in Holland, and probably identical with a thousand Mimosa Streets. Tiny two-storied houses in two neat bricky rows, patterned into little parcels of six at a time. One saw through the huge windows to a further street, and through that again to infinity. Exactly like the Droste cocoa-tin. Painted on it is a nurse, holding another cocoa-tin, with a nurse on it . . .

Miniature balconies with iron railings, over the front door; miniature gardens with a few bulbs and a strip of grass. A grass verge between path and roadway. When I got home there were already four Volkswagens standing neatly parked. All the houses are identical; I wondered which was mine. The Mimosa Street is Holland.

I stopped for a gaze; Van der Valk's brooding, piercing, aquiline look; Michelangelo contemplating Saint Peter's.

I probably looked struck with amnesia, paralysis of the motor nerves, or perhaps just as though I had a rick in the back.

A child's scooter was flung against the verge; two families had not yet taken in their dustbins. A little girl had tied a string to a fence, and was holding the free end very solemnly and seriously, watching another little girl jumping over it in a complicated, important procession of steps. A bigger girl, in tartan trousers she had grown out of, was roller-skating with the sudden ducking lurch and widespread fingers of the beginner, watched with admiration by two tiny ones in woolly tights. Very pink cheeks and naughty eyes peeping out of the hoods of their windcheaters; moisture forming on curls in front; bright Norwegian mittens; one was rather bow-legged.

Others could gaze too; I felt the pressure of twenty pairs of unseen eyes going prickling over the skin on the back of my neck. I locked the car door, picked up the good brief-case and scampered for my door; crinkle glass badly set in flimsy softwood painted a depressing yellow.

The muslin glass-curtains of the house across the street flickered as I turned to shut the door. Those eyes were able to count the stitches that darned my left sock last week.

There was a good smell of pot-on-the-fire; celery, leeks, turnips, onions puttering gently. Arlette was gazing fascinated at German children's television; the film had been dubbed, and one had the charming effect of an English copper, pot hat and all, out in the midday sun but talking forthright Kölner German. She had bought a plant; a feathery little coco-palm fluttered in the draught and I shut the room door hastily.

'I've been writing to the boys, telling them all the frightful things that are happening to us. And I bought some smoked eel. We're going to have a nice evening – *Cosí Fan Tutte* from the new theatre in Frankfurt.'

Which pleased me very much. I wasn't in a thinking mood.

Tomorrow, anyway, was only a boring trek round pastures a lot of oxen had nibbled pretty bare.

## 3

The next morning was bright and sunny. Even in westerly weather it is often so in Holland. It is a false promise, for already before midday a grey pall of cloud will have blanketed the sky, a cold little wind will be searching the bones at street corners, stirring up dust, and presently rain will turn the dust again to mud. But while it lasts, the sunshine cheers everybody. It has the thin, bright texture of morning, and accompanies a whole happy orchestra of morning noises. Loud crash of dustbins being emptied into the creeping garbage lorry, a strange animal that digests suburban refuse by standing on its head and then yawns toothily for more. The clattering three-wheeler of the milkman, seeming far too burdened for its very tiny, incredibly noisy motor. The milkman sits upon this poor beast wearing an extraordinary sort of Australian bush hat against the elements, and scribbles busily in his little book as he bumps over the uneven brick; total mystery how it can be legible even to him. Presently he will jump off, bang lustily on a bell that came off the Inchcape Rock, and pretend to be a Caribbean Steel Band, exactly as though he had come creepy-creepy on slippers and now wanted to give the housewives a start.

Building sites give whoops on their hooters, telling workmen who are already, probably, flat on their backs playing cards – strange how workmen seem the same all over the world; Tired Tim and Weary Willy – that they can have a coffee-break. There is an uproar from school playgrounds where the children – also the same everywhere – shriek in a thin, piercing tone that is also very much a morning noise.

In the falsely genial shopping street, I felt, in the Volkswagen, like a Mexican on his donkey. Housewives riding bikes, pushing bikes, lugging tiny children off the backs of bikes – all in the middle of the road and paying not the least attention either to me in a tiny blackbeetle auto or to Albert Heijn's lorry, which is ten feet tall and thirty long. They are busy with the shopping. They stand in the middle of the road, staring at the bargains-of-the-day, announced on bits of cardboard propped against a condensed-milk pyramid; shouting red, and mis-spelt. There are unheard-of, unrepeatable unique opportunities to get two pieces of soap and a toothbrush, all free if one just buys two of the new giant-pack boxes. Are housewives, I wondered, more naïve than usual when the sun shines? There was a broad-beamed soul sticking well out into the road, a globular toddler with its eyes popping out clutched in her muscular armpit, forcing a cabbage into her bicycle-pannier. She glared rather, as though it were my fault that she couldn't get it in. Perhaps she would now try clutching the cabbage and stuffing the toddler.

This was Drente too, but I didn't think it was the real Drente. It looked identical with everywhere else in Holland, and could just as easily have been the Jan van Galenstraat in Amsterdam-West. Housewives with anonymous pieces of meat, neatly squeezed into a plastic pillow-case that makes any ragged old strip of trek-ox look succulent and as though it deserved to be so expensive. A quarter of liver-sausage and a quarter of soapy cheese, both cut very thin on the bacon-slicer, and a packet of smelly biscuits for this afternoon with the tea.

I got stuck behind another vast lorry, containing, to judge from huge curly letters written on it, nothing but several million jelly-babies. But at last I was at the top. I disregarded the one tree-shaded road in Zwinderen, where the houses of the managerial class are – interesting though this was – and went on past the railway station and the milk factory next door. Here a road, broad and bare, brand new, had been driven into the soggy countryside. It had no pavements, but a wide, bricked bicycle-path on each side. This was the 'Industry Terrain'. No houses here, but neat factories on both sides, prim, quiet and abandoned-looking. More lorries standing like oxen with their trailers behind them. A goods truck on a spur line standing by a loading platform, and two overalled characters languidly stacking cardboard crates. Through the fields behind ran the canal, and a faint noise reached me from where a suction line was unloading sand and gravel barges for the Readymixed Konkrete Co. (Shouldn't that be Ko.?)

I reached the electronics factory and parked the auto where it said 'Executives Only', outside a towering wall of glass window through which nothing could be seen at all. There was a loud smell of packing materials from a loading bay; corrugated cardboard and gummed sealing strip and stencilling ink. A notice told me to State my Business at the Timekeeper's Office, which adjoined a shed full of non-executive bikes.

Three minutes later I was being ushered into the owner-director's office. Not as lucky as it sounds; I had found out from Miss Burger that he had regular days.

'What can I do for you, Mr Uh? From The Hague, I see. Ethnographic Survey, huh?' – brightly and a little cunningly, as though he knew all about those surveys.

'Yes. We are naturally anxious to follow all the uh, trends that may be situated by setting up industry here. Housing, transport, leisure activities of workers, uh, retail outlets.' Splendid phrase; I was not quite sure what it meant.

'Quite, quite. And how can I help you? You want to interview the personnel or something?'

I leaned forward with a sharp disapproving nose. 'This conversation is confidential and inviolable.' He looked startled, as I had intended. He was one of these knowing businessmen with a hoarse chuckling voice.

'Certainly, if you wish. We're quite undisturbed here.'

I passed one of my real cards across the desk and enjoyed the reaction.

'Inspector . . . Central Recherche . . . what's this about? I've made no complaint; we've had no troubles; as far as I know we've broken no laws.'

'Glad to hear it, but I'm interested neither in peculation nor the maximum agreed wage – I'm interested in the death of your technical director's wife.'

'Oh my god . . . you mean this ethnographic hooha is . . .?'

'In this town I am an official of the Ministry of the Interior; I mean to stay that way. There've been more than enough policemen already.'

'How I agree. Poor Betty. But I fail to see –'

'You aren't under any suspicion. This is verbal, informal, confidential, just like my own identity. Whatever you may say is not stenographed.'

'But I've told the police anything I knew – precious little, incidentally.'

I believe in pushing, when possible, this kind of person off balance.

'I should like you to tell me the things you've suppressed in previous meetings with the police,' pleasantly.

'I've suppressed nothing, damn it.'

'Generally called forgetting – often truly, at that. I'm not calling you a liar, but this affair concerns the life of everyone in this town.'

'But not mine, man.'

'Everyone.'

'Damn it, I don't even live here. I come here two days, maybe three, a week. Reinders lives here. He's the man you want.'

'But I chose to start with you. You stay the night here, sometimes?'

'Well, it has been known, when Will and I were working on a problem.'

'And where, then? Not in a hotel?'

'Well, no; they're ghastly.'

'At Will's house, no? Normal, natural, understandable – and much more comfortable.'

'I'm not trying to conceal it,' defensively.

'You called her Betty, equally naturally.'

'You've no objection, I hope.'

'Quite the contrary, I'm delighted. Ever sleep with her?'

That got to him. Business man, flabbergasted.

'Don't give yourself the trouble of looking shocked.'

He hoisted the expression off the floor and wrestled with it a moment. A small smile crept out.

'Well . . . I was just thinking that the last set of policemen turned round that very question without quite daring to ask it, and you come plump straight out. The answer is no. And what's more she was a very conscientious woman and I don't believe the boy-friend did either.'

'Why exactly did you give him the bullet, since as I understood there was no great gossip or scandal caused?'

'In the first place, because he wasn't a particularly good craftsman. Second, because Will didn't.'

'Will, I take it, thought it wouldn't be fair.'

'Put it this way. Will wasn't going to stand for the fellow hanging about Betty and to give him the push – it might be said he had acted out of personal motives, even spite. Whereas coming from me . . . I simply told the chap he wasn't giving the ability to his work that justified my paying him that much. Betty, poor innocent, thought Will knew nothing about it.'

'What amuses me is that neither you nor Will are above pinching a handy bottom on a trip, but at the mildest indiscretion of the wife you're all remarkably drastic.'

'We're extremely careful to cause no trouble or gossip anywhere near our homes,' curtly.

I had got the background I wanted. The two husbands, gifted, energetic, often abroad and accustomed to a circle of others equally thrusting, had played the part expected of them. Whisky and call-girls in the hotelsuites of Düsseldorf or Milan. Half the fun was in kicking over the respectability to which they were constrained at home. The girls had meant no more than a stolen apple. Betty, a small-town, strictly-reared girl, had had intoxicating tastes of these men's conversation and jokes. She had got over her initial prudery and tried to keep up with them. Stuck at home, a bit neglected by a husband giving too much time to his career, having no children, she had done a few innocent, mildly silly things, but had had the bad luck to be spied out by a blackmailer who had enormously magnified it all. The tangle had grown involved, she had dreaded causing a scandal, dreaded compromising her husband's position, and had not been able to ride the squall out. Neither the experience of life nor the firmness of character. Who knows: she had perhaps given in to the blackmailer's demands. Finally, she had seen nothing for it but sleeping pills.

'That was how it happened – you agree?'

'Yes; I rather think so, seen like that. But if only she'd told Will – or me, come to that. We'd have backed her up, of course.'

Prodding this character off balance had been a success; I decided to try a second barrel and a riskier shot.

'One more small point. Your firm produces sensitive listening gadgets for various purposes. There's a lot of mention in the police reports of one that might have been useful in a blackmailer's hands. The thing that – what does it do?'

'Listens to machinery, jet engines to take an example, under test. It can detect faint flutters with a high level of exterior noise. I know what you're heading at; it's nonsense.'

'You maintained that no such apparatus could get into the wrong hands.'

'I did and I do.'

'You don't have to tell me lies, you know. Don't interrupt. You, and Will, occasionally take things home. Prototypes or whatever you call them. You play with them at home, and you may think up a modification or experiment on an improvement. Right?'

'Well, that's so, within limits, but . . .'

'Now it occurred to you – just as it occurred to me; I wasn't born yesterday either – that it might be very comic to try one of these things out in a hotel, say? You did, and found it a good joke, and being a big broadminded business man you had a good laugh about this in Betty's presence. Am I wrong?'

'Completely.'

'Nonsense,' in an unimpressed way. 'You left a gadget – I don't say this one, but some similar bit of apparatus – lying about in Will's house. When it disappeared you didn't even notice at first. When you did you were alarmed because the thing is classified as secret. After Betty's death you were really scared, because it occurred to you that this thing might in some way be connected. And you stuck to a lie through thick and thin. This is all logical, natural, consequential. But you've just denied it with such false bravado, and you are looking so particularly guilty, that I know that this – ach, not necessarily in detail – is so.'

'But my god . . . how do you know?'

'I guessed. Look, the writer of these letters boasts of being the ear of God. That is a figurative remark; the fact is, however, that this person knows a remarkable number of things that an ordinary person would not know. The conclusion is that he got something of this sort, and presumably from or through Betty. I'm not accusing you. Now tell me about the thing – what it looks like; how it's used.'

'It's in a cigar-box,' much squashed, even shaken. 'We chose that to act as a model for the size of unit we wanted.

We've managed to reduce the size since, but in essentials it's unchanged. It's like a transistor set – with special valves of course. It has two loop aerials that act as direction finders, give a cross bearing, and can pinpoint a sound. It's powered by ordinary transistor batteries. It has ear-phones with baffles that shut out exterior sound. They weren't perfected, but at night, or anywhere with no more than an ordinary volume of sound . . . you only have to focus it on a wall or something, and choose the right distance and angle. If you get too close you might get overriding sounds on the same bearing – I mean from further off the angle's more acute and the bearing more precise. At about thirty feet you'd get a conversation like ours.'

'So you were badly scared.'

'We thought it might get used for espionage or something. Anybody could learn to use it with a little practice. Of course it's classified; we have a model for commercial use that works at much closer quarters only, can be built into inspection units. The Ministry would kick up a great stink . . . When Betty died, and then they found those letters we . . . some policeman got the idea but we were able to deny it.'

'We'll get it back; it's not being used for espionage. But just as long as we understand each other. I can twist your arm. You say nothing, you hear? About this, or about me. And not even to Will. You breathe and I'll break your neck with this.'

I stopped on the way out, and gave him my lecherous grin.

# 4

The sun had vanished as I came out, and there was a raw north-westerly wind. I had still another call to make: the manager of the milk co-operative. His office here was not private, but the house adjoining was his home and I decided to work on him there. He was quite a classic type for stiffness and conformity. I certainly did not suspect him of anything, but there were one or two things in the reports I had thought a little odd, and I had wondered whether I could use these to lever any interesting information out of him.

I had to wait five minutes; he had, it appeared, 'some instructions he had to give'. The kitchen-maid put me in the good front room, and there I amused myself while waiting.

I was hunting for an elusive phrase in my mind, and caught the reference suddenly. Ernest Hemingway. Over-rated writer, but he wrote one good book at least, and created some unforgettable characters. This man was like one of them ... Hemingway, of course, had been talking about a Spaniard. What were the exact words? 'Heavier than mercury; fuller of boredom than a steer drawing a cart on a country road.' Fernando, in *Bell* – peculiarly apt for this personage.

You saw it looking round the room. It was classic too; the provincial 'good front room' of the Holland of forty years ago. Where no one ever came, bar the dominie twice a year, and the relations for the wedding anniversary, and the daughters for their protocolaire piano-practising. Sad rooms, hatefully clean, revoltingly arranged and undisturbed, full of unseen shutters, reeking of must and fust. Not one single tiny object that was either beautiful or useful; not a scrap of fringe or varnish that was necessary. No spontaneous, unpretentious breath had ever been drawn here.

Why had the woman who had lived in this house put her head in the gas-oven? Looking at this room, I could hardly believe that she had made even the trivial slip that put her in the hands of a blackmailer. Something, I thought, had threatened her 'standing'. Her position of ease and assurance among the other wives on the good-works committee; most precious thing in her life. Something had so undermined that solid prop that she had lost her footing and gone under. Provincial Holland.

The steer came into the room, fidgeted, and sat at last uneasily on a plush chair. This was the only room where one could be sure that the kitchen-maid would not be able to listen.

They had given out that the wife had had an incurable disease. He had been much sympathized with, the good man. Perhaps he would marry again, as soon as standing and provincial morality approved.

I took one of my real cards out slowly.

'I am here on the instructions of the Procureur-Général. This whole business must be cleared up.'

'It has nothing whatever to do with me.'

'Your wife, alas, died.'

'Whatever it is that you are investigating, uh – Inspector, I would prefer you to stop these attempts to drag my wife's memory into disrepute.'

'Ah. I quite understand. You would prefer it if nothing more was ever said or done. Unfortunately, I'm going through with this, regardless of whatever must be disturbed or uncovered.'

Good heavens, how the fellow sat, encrusted in virtue. I'd really like to tell him he deserves pelting with stale eggs for producing such lousy milk. Look at him – rancid as his own butter.

Now that won't do. I must not allow these things to affect me. My feelings about butter are not relevant to the death of a poor wretch's unhappy wife.

'I'll do everything I can to spare you pain or publicity. You see that I have come anonymously, and very likely I'll never worry you again. But this is like a creeping sepsis – we really must cut deep. These frightened little prods at the surface only make things worse.'

It seemed to have no effect. Fellow sat there like a bump

on a log, correct, humourless, righteous. I felt as though I were wading through toffee, and ploughed heavily.

'This is a judicial inquiry; you are legally required to answer my questions. Now – correct me if these details are wrong, which I quote from official police reports. When you found your wife, you immediately locked the whole house, you went in person to the police, and you asked for the inspector in person. You refused to speak to the uniformed agent. You did not telephone. You appeared at the bureau at eight-ten in the morning; you waited twenty minutes for the inspector and you insisted that he come, alone.'

'That is correct.'

'Why did you not call a doctor?'

'I knew that it would serve no purpose. My wife had been exposed too long to the poisonous effects of gas. I opened the windows; I locked the doors, not only because the cleaning woman was due to arrive and might have been exposed to danger, but because it was no affair of hers.'

'How did you know how long your wife had been exposed?'

'She had been in bed. I heard her go downstairs. I told the inspector that.'

He had; it was in the report. She had gone down at night in her pyjamas, when the husband was awake, or had at least wakened.

Had she hoped that he would find her, stop her? I felt that he didn't know – that she had perhaps chosen this as a way of telling him. But he had fallen asleep without waiting for her to return.

A poignant aspect of the whole thing was that not only is a gas-oven death a rarity in Holland; the gas-oven itself is a rarity. The Dutch scarcely use ovens in their cooking. This had been another example of provincial pretentiousness – an imposing gas-stove, whose oven had never once been used.

Why then had she used it now–for the first, the only time? How had she heard that this is a suicide method? In England, now, it is common, and reported in the Press, but she would not have known that. Had she really put her own head in the oven? Or had she been put? The State Recherche had considered this too, but as with the other questionable points, no clear conclusion could be reached.

The man was still sitting unmoved.

'Tell me – why go to see the inspector? Why not ring your doctor, and let him see to the formalities? He could have made the statutory notification to the police.'

'As everybody found quite natural, Inspector, I was upset. I suppose I thought that in a case of suicide . . .'

'Is your doctor not a friend of yours?'

'Certainly he is.'

'Is he no good?'

'I have complete confidence in him.'

'I rather thought you had. He suggested – or at least concurred in this invention of a disease. Whereas there was no disease. We know – and you know – that your wife was perfectly healthy. Therefore, I think, you went to the inspector. Saying, "Come quick". Yet you claim that you know nothing about the letters some people have received – or that there had been another suicide, fairly recently at that, under circumstances that were fairly mysterious too, or so the village gossip ran.'

'I know nothing about letters, and I do not listen to gossip. I have since been told that certain persons appear to have received anonymous letters, but it has never been proved that my wife was among them. And you have no right to insinuate that she was.'

'Have *you* had any letters?'

'No. As I have told the other officers. And I fail to see what purpose this repetition will serve.'

'You can just leave me to be the judge of that. I am in authority here.'

It squashed him. These people are scared sick of their government.

'Well, I intended no discourtesy . . .'

'You still maintain that it was normal to leave your wife lying on the kitchen floor, while you ran for the inspector – even waiting twenty minutes for him, refusing to give any details to the staff on duty?'

Not even this reached a target. He just sat, prissily.

'The inspector is an acquaintance; it seemed to me natural that my contact should be with someone I knew could be relied on.'

'Relied on not to gossip?'

Hell, what could I do to penetrate? I knew it wasn't right; it didn't sound right. This fellow knew about the letters – I was damn sure of it. But how to make him spill?

Well, with the other, the engineer, a thrust had disarmed, laid open. But that was at least a highly intelligent man, and not a provincial. This man is lowish on intelligence. I decided to take the stick. Make a crude smash through all the careful defences and hedges of propriety.

'Just tell me one thing.'

'If I can, naturally,' very stiff.

'Have you ever done anything that would give a person – any person – the smallest opening to make an accusation, to your wife or yourself? An accusation of immorality?'

Looked as though slapped with a wet, stinking floor-cloth.

'Most certainly and decidedly not.'

'Never?' sweetly. I picked rough, direct phrases; street-words. 'These nice bits you have there in the white overalls; never kissed one of them? Never craftily sort of slid your hand up a skirt when no one was looking? Or that kitchen-maid – fresh, young, nice white teeth. Quite appetizing in that tight skirt. You could quietly slip the pants off that behind the ice-box door; nobody would know.'

Outrage, looking like a dying cod.

'How dare you – how can you – I would never dream – I swear to you – never never never – such filth – obscenity from the mouth of an official – it's unthinkable.'

It had worked. That was truth at least.

'But the letters accused you of these things,' I said cheerfully. The poor bugger stopped dead.

'But I destroyed all the letters.'

'Now we're getting somewhere.'

'Oh . . .'

I thought myself a dirty stinker, to play such an old low trick on a sanctified cheesemonger.

I drilled in for half an hour, and was ready to bet at the end that he was telling the truth. He had not dreamed – well, he might have dreamed but had certainly not dared. Not only had the wife's sharp eyes been on godliness (next to cleanliness) but a hundred other vinegary hawk-eyes . . . Avoid the very appearance of evil – I could hear the dominie, mellifluously. Ironically, the same one that had been accused of having naughty photos.

Yet, even here, these things were done; even in the smallest, primmest places. They had been done at Staphorst. And last year, in just such another enclosed, schismatic dorp, the accusation I had just made had been made too, and against a minister. By another minister.

The court had decided it was not true, and minister number one had caught a sharpish rap for defamation. But it didn't matter whether it were true or not. Such accusations had only to be made to be, already, effective. There would certainly be elderly saints ready to believe all this and more.

Just so here. These accusations were quite likely, even probably, not true at all. But the blackmailer had known they would be most efficacious. Whoever it was, it was someone who thoroughly understood the workings of villages.

This chap, I felt sufficiently sure, was telling the truth and had not strayed. And wasn't that just what caught him, as it had caught the wife? The sheer enormity of being accused of straying had paralysed them. They had known that the very appearance of evil would ruin them.

# 5

I went to see the burgomaster that evening for the first time since coming. At his home, in the evening, by arrangement. I left the Volkswagen a street away, deliberately, and walked to the pleasant house, almost a villa, on the Koninginne-weg, Queen Street. There is a Koninginneweg in every town in Holland, just like the Mimosastraat. It is grander, that is all the difference. There are trees. Houses of the bourgeois. Doctors, dentists, notaries, bank managers, burgomasters. Was it the Mimosastraat that would be the most important, here?

A pleasure to be able to make verbal reports, in language as brief and colloquial as I cared to make it. I was even quite an almighty personage here; I could puncture the burgomaster's evening and make any one of fifteen thousand people shake in his shoes. Which I couldn't do in Amsterdam!

I thought that I preferred, on the whole, being a small fish that looks very small indeed in a very big pond. Still, to be free of reports was nice. I am accustomed, heaven bear witness, to written reports – they are seven-tenths of a policeman's life. I am even good at them, but I've never got over detesting them.

I was received by the wife. Pretty woman, a bit artificially blonde. With the wrong make-up she would have looked thoroughly vulgar, but she had been very careful with clothes and face and voice. Lady of the manor, but ever so unspoilt and charming when receiving flowers from little girls. I instantly saw her cutting the ribbon for the orphanage's new wing, and did not care greatly for her at first sight. She looked at me as though I were a lavatory attendant, drunk on duty at that.

'I'm afraid you cannot – you must ask for an appointment in writing.'

I supposed it was the maid's day off.

'Just give him my card if you will be so good.' I still got a disapproving look for not knowing my place. I watched her walk away with more pleasure. Clothes a bit offensively Christian, but nice legs and a certain allure from the back. Van der Valk – blow your nose, and avoid lechery.

Burgomaster appeared, in rather self-conscious television-undress of tweed jacket and woolly slippers.

'Of course, of course. Er – I'm sorry, Ansje, this is business of importance and confidential. Come into my study – er, Mr van der Valk.'

He fussed a bit, wondering whether to be genial, or whether to be the superior official, on the frigid side. Decided to be genial. More tactful.

'Er – perhaps a glass of sherry?'

'Many thanks.'

'There we are. And – what progress have you made, so far? I realize these are early days. Is your house adequate, by the way?'

'Yes, thank you. Your admirable secretary filled all the gaps and even got some things my wife forgot; I was most grateful to her.'

'Ah yes; Miss Burger's splendid; admirable is the word; she knows how to get hold of anything. So – you're not too dissatisfied, with your start?'

'Sure I'm dissatisfied.'

'Oh.' Wind taken out of municipal sails, a scrap. 'But you've reached some fruitful conclusions? Suspects, for instance; you've succeeded in isolating some suggestive uh, discoveries?'

'There aren't any suspects, so I can't isolate any. Unless

you mean in the sense that everyone is suspect, even yourself.'

'Ah – quite.'

'I'm isolating victims. Indeed the author of these crimes, disturbances – call it what you will – is a victim. Someone unable to resist pressure.'

'I hope,' earnestly, 'you're not in danger of taking an over – what shall I call it – metaphysical viewpoint, Inspector? When can we all be reassured that an end is being made? I do agree that the mental state of this uh, author will give psychiatrists a headache. But is that the most fruitful ground for your approach?'

'I haven't any approach. But everybody spent months hunting for suspects – I still think there's more to be learned from the victims.'

'Can you give me no concrete reassurances, though – based on what you've seen and done, these – three isn't it? – days?'

'Certainly. We'll soon run this amorous letter-writer to earth, burgomaster; you can be reassured. And I don't even think the field of inquiry will prove to be all that large. Further than that I would not like to go yet.'

'Excellent. By the way, have you yourself formed any opinion about our friend Besançon?'

'Yes indeed. I've met him. I like him very much.'

'You don't think yourself that he's involved in any way?'

'Not for a minute. Except that he's a victim too, of course.'

'I suppose so. Naturally, that terrible history would lead anybody into feeling deep sympathy for such a man, and yet who knows what goes on in the head of a man who has seen the things he has?'

It was the first sensible remark I had heard from him, and I looked at him with proper respect.

# 6

'How d'you get on?' Arlette asked sympathetically.

'Oh, I smeared him with jam. When he got jam on his eyelids and between his fingers, and couldn't pester me any more, I shoved a bit down his throat and left him to enjoy it. He's all right; only wants reassurance.'

'I'm glad to see you're feeling better.'

'I go round like Father Brown, being enigmatical and paradoxical. And now I could do with a drink; I got thimblefuls of sherry doled out to me.'

I am not, I am grateful to say, the least like James Bond. Don't have hanging locks of hair, don't kill people – not, that is to say, quite that many – am not very British, and am left unmoved by passionate women with eccentric names. Not even a muddied oaf and a flannelled fool – I am simply a clot in a ready-made suit. But I do like large cold expensive drinks in large cold expensive glasses. Here's to you, Bond; may your sexual capacities never grow less. But do be careful, old boy; don't ever tap yourself on the head with the emerald Fabergé spoon, thinking you're a boiled egg in a four-and-a-half-litre Bentley egg-cup.

'You ought to get that Miss Burger to see about finding me a fridge,' said Arlette. 'Don't eat all the salt biscuits; I haven't had any yet.'

# 7

I woke up in deep gloom and knew it was going to be one of those days. The coffee was revolting, the weather beastly, the windscreen wipers were on the blink all day, and when

I got home Arlette had (a) forgotten to put the dustbin out, (b) forgotten that it was early closing day.

Still, that was all unimportant. Things like this happened to Rembrandt too. What worried me the whole day was not understanding a damn thing about provincial towns in Drente. Serve me right. Puffed up with braggadocio, thinking all the other policemen were imbeciles. The elaborate disguise, the calculated politenesses and rudeness, the vaunted urban sophistications . . . pooh.

I was a vain, tattle-mouthed dolt.

I knew nothing.

I understood nothing.

When you meet the unorthodox, meet it in an unorthodox way. Pooh – with froth on top.

I was sitting in Monsieur Cousteau's bathyscaphe, exploring the great silent wonders of the submarine world. Suddenly I noticed a signboard; neat white paint on shiny blue enamel. Very common, in Holland.

'You are now standing at the exact geographical centre of the Gobi Desert,' it said admonishingly. 'No admittance for unauthorized persons (Article 436 of the Code of Criminal Law).'

I looked out of my copper-bound crystal window. Damn it, they were dead right. I am out of my depth, I told myself wittily.

I went home and was curt with Arlette, till she got fed up with it.

'Look, I agree that we've both eaten better meals, but there's nothing wrong with this dinner even if it is mostly out of boxes. Will you please stop being disagreeable – or at least tell me what's eating you. You're depressed, I can see – but why don't you tell me?'

'Because I make it a rule not to, as you know very well, and also because you intensely dislike hearing about these things.'

'Listen. We're together here. We're alone. This place, this

70

house, whatever it is, has been wished on me as well as on you.' She thought, hard. 'We're just going to stack these dishes. Sit down over there. Pour me out a glass of Ashtray.' This is her name for a sort of German marc whose full title goes 'Asbach-Uralt-is-the-soul-of-the-wine'. Being French, she feels it her duty to be comic about this, but I notice she enjoys drinking it.

I heard Arlette throw all the washing-up in the sink. I then heard her go upstairs, change her frock, comb her hair, repair her paint and go to the lavatory.

Not only was I unaccustomed to the lack of privacy in a small suburban house, but I was outraged at the loss of dignity it implied. The whole street, I thought viciously, can hear and has apparently to know every detail of my wife's everyday existence. Things that aren't even my business. I find this revolting.

She had changed into a wool frock, a soft dusty buttercuppy colour that I was fond of. She smelt good; I wished, as I do every day, that I could give up smoking and get a better nose. Taste things, and deposit them politely in a silver spittoon. A tea-blender – that would make a splendid job for Van der Valk.

'I hate crimes, yes,' she said, holding the lighter up to the cigarette in her mouth. 'Hate murders, and all ghastly gory details. But I can't really see that whatever's been going on here is much of a crime.'

'If you put moral pressure on people till they feel there's no way out but to kill themselves, it's as much of a murder as a plastic bomb.'

'I suppose, yes. But isn't it society that is the murderer more than the person? Environment or whatever. If I've understood, people killed themselves for fear of the public, for fear of newspapers, what people will say ... In other words they can't stand the pressure of existence. What difference is there between them and someone who kills herself because of an unhappy love affair – the girl who is

71

pregnant and feels abandoned by everybody, say? The man who drinks and can no longer keep a job – or – oh, anything. Go on, tell me.'

'You are my resource against depression, aren't you?' I was touched.

'And isn't that my job?'

'I find you a thoroughly nice woman.'

'Now tell me what is getting you down?'

'Being a foreigner. I've never felt so conscious of it in my life. Not in France or even England.'

'You? But I'm the foreigner. You're the one who's Dutch. Sometimes you're even very Dutch,' grinning.

'Not here.' Van der Valk; one deep sigh.

A drink of Ash-tray lent me some sort of spurious energy.

'I came across a file of reports. Brief notes on police court cases, annotated by a judge. Pointing out that people from this part are emigrants in Holland – in the metroland, I mean, our way. They're still in their own country, but they're strangers. They seem to have a higher percentage of petty indictments brought against them than the home product. This judge formed a theory, and wrote a memo on it to the Ministry. That they feel both inferior and lonely. Deduction, the indictments are due to a sort of crude bravado – compensation feelings. You follow?'

'I follow, but I'm not sure I understand.'

'Simply, this is a foreign country. When they come racing down and get south, say, of Amersfoort, they find that nobody understands their language, the food is different, the ideas are different, there's Catholics and all sorts of other riff-raff, and they are just looked on as having crawled straight out of the bog. But here the boot is on the other foot. We're the bloody foreigners, they resent us and they kick. Every way they can. They cheat even – I've been diddled out of threepenny bits a dozen times already.'

'I've noticed that, but I thought they were penny-pinchers because they were poor.'

'Qué, poor.'

'They've been terribly poor for generations. One doesn't get it out of the blood so quickly.'

'I don't believe it. I think one forgets quick enough, and they're all dripping with it now.'

'The ground has a lot to do with it. Bad ground. Just like in the Haute Savoie.'

'I don't think that's quite everything. It's a religious thing too. These queer parts of countries are different in more ways. You look at the figures Larousse gives for the different departments of France on cases of alcoholism, mental disease, congenital deformity, as well as the poverty diseases like TB. Sharp jump upwards in the backwoods territories – Savoie, Morbihan, parts of Languedoc. Same here, I'll bet. I think they feel apart, they feel persecuted, and feel hatred for the occupying army. Why should strangers come here and get rich? Skin them, every chance you get. Skin the brethren too, by all means, but that's part of the game – they know the rules. But common front against the outsiders. Of course there are more and more outsiders, and they can't go on for ever, but they're keeping up a rear-guard action.'

'You're feeling that.'

'And how.'

'Are the people who suffer from the letters strangers?'

'It's an interesting point; I'll have to study it. But I can't find out how many people have had letters. They won't open their mouths unless I happen to know a way of twisting their arm ... Sometimes I get the feeling that all the accusations are imaginary; no basis behind the whole thing.'

'Tell me.'

'I mean that the author of the letters is just making a witch-hunt. Popular hysteria feeds on this, and is now ready to believe the worst of anybody and everybody. If the burgomaster, to take an example, now got letters accusing him of something frightful or just shameful – with no atom of truth in it at all – people would make an outcry against him. It's explosive, this; that's why I've got to stop it. You can feel that people are jumpy, uneasy. Ready to throw accusations, and listen to them seriously. At anyone, however respected. Like at Salem. Did you read that book?'

'*The Devil in Massachusetts?*' with relish. 'Yes, fascinating.'

'There wasn't any witch, but they constructed dozens. Teenage girls saw and heard and felt witches all over the shop.'

'The people had very hard dreary lives, and a rigid puritan code of ethics.'

'See any resemblance?'

'Yes, I suppose so. But as far as I could see the girls just invented witches to make life more amusing and exciting. They had no newspapers, no radio, television, trains, shops, cinemas. They've all that, here.'

'Yes, but that's not quite what I meant. Those girls had a vague but strong feeling of guilt, that everything exciting and amusing was caused by the devil and therefore witchcraft. There were witches, in the people's minds. There I think the parallel is better.'

'They hung a lot of innocent people to get rid of the feeling of themselves being guilty – the fear of becoming witches themselves, or even already being witches.'

'Exactly. By the girls' accounts, every damned last one of them was a witch. They weren't having that, of course.'

I found myself enthusiastically pouring in another drink and discovered that I had forgotten my depression. Arlette's therapy . . .

'It's something, though, they need to cure locally. To call in an outsider, like me – mistake. They make resolute common front against me here.'

'There's witchcraft on the bloody milk here, all right,' remarked Arlette frivolously.

# 8

In the middle of the night I got an idea. The whole street, I had thought in a loud indignant bellow, can hear and has apparently to know every detail of my wife's daily existence.

Why shouldn't I – or my wife – turn the tables? Take a passionate interest in the whole street's daily existence. The way they did themselves. Shadow-watching and all the rest.

I could certainly sit all day bird-watching with a pair of binoculars, just the way the letter-writer did. Like dirty old men in parks. Fascinating; something I had always wanted to do.

I recalled a visit I had once paid to an English wartime comrade, who lives in Bristol. He went to Cambridge after his demob and is now an architect. Intelligent, delightful man. He complained about the dreadful provincialism of Bristol, but admitted that the huge wooded park at the north side – The Downs, they call it – was wonderful.

'Wonderful place for lover-watching,' he had said, amusedly. 'We have a little park in the town too. It's nothing – just a sort of bare hill. For some extraordinary reason the lovers there are quite shameless. The local boys have a perfect name for it.'

'What is it?' I was fascinated.

'They call it "taking a piece up Mutton Tump".'

'Mutton Tump?'

'You Dutch. Etymology is really quite simple. Tump is a genuine old word for a bare hill of some sort. Mutton – have you already forgotten that in the army we used to say, of such and such a girl, nurse, waaf, whatever she was, "That one hawks her mutton"?'

Mutton Tump! I had been enchanted.

The trouble was that I simply didn't have time. In Amsterdam I could have called on an auxiliary. Here I was alone. These middle-of-the-night ideas, I thought, falling asleep again; they never do stand up to daylight.


# 9


'Are you really interested?' I asked at breakfast. Good coffee, this morning; the sun was shining too.

'I almost think I am.'

'Would you like to help me?'

'How on earth can I help you?' She was astonished. What did she know about crimes – or witches, come to that.

'You can help me a great deal.'

'But what can I do?'

The Mimosastraat is Holland, and this particularly Mimosa Street is Drente.

'I want you to be one of the housewives that spend all day looking out of their windows.'

'I'm more likely to be canonized as a second Jeanne d'Arc.'

'Yes I know, but that's all wrong. We are just making them more suspicious of you and me. Have you exchanged a word with any of them?'

'A distant good morning.'

'You see? Now we're reacting by being defensive. Wrong tactics. You don't have to be pally, but talk to them, gossip with them. I don't ask you to invite them all in to drink coffee and borrow the grass-mower, but don't be stiff or stuck-up. Let them find out you're human even if you are a queer French cow. Talk about the washing and the dusting and the price of cabbage. And above all, watch. Watch every slightest tiny little thing. And listen. However poisonous, malicious, idle or stupid it seems to be, hang on to it and write it down; it may prove to be exactly what I want.

'You know,' thoughtfully, holding out my cup for more

coffee; in the early morning, thoughtfulness depends a good deal on coffee – 'I'm supposed to be making an ethnographic study; I may as well take that quite seriously. The better I play the part, the sooner we'll be out of this.'

'I'll do my best,' dubiously. 'I can't see myself exchanging jollities with the wives over the wash-line, our mouths full of clothes-pegs. But I've little enough to do, with no boys, and I can sit with a little notebook.'

'You'll be surprised how easy it is. Remember, they'll be fair bursting with curiosity about you.'

Arlette didn't find it difficult. She trotted out with her clothes-pegs, and smiled agreeably at the nearest wife, busily pinning a back garden away. This was a brisk person, with the quick nervous movements of the housewife, sharp eyes behind her glasses and a penetrating voice. She responded instantly with the classic gambit.

'Lovely day for drying.'

Arlette found her abominably nosy, a master of the point-blank question that is rude anywhere else, but not in Holland.

But she was just as ready to give confidences. It is indeed the hallmark of the suburban street neither to have secrets from your neighbours nor to find sharing theirs at all unusual. Arlette was cross-examined closely, and found it difficult work, but the oddity of her ideas could be put down to being French. She forced herself to be voluble about her children, the horrors of other people's furniture, the income and pension of government functionaries, and the utter wickedness of adding yet another cent to the retail price of margarine. In return she heard all about the daughter that was a nurse, the daughter still at the 'household school', and the boy who was the same age as Arlette's eldest – oh, these boys. Difficult . . . French or not, they had plenty of common ground.

Mrs Tattle, as Arlette christened her promptly, finished the delicate work of pinning up her husband's Sunday white shirt, leaned burly, mottled arms across the fence, and told blissfully all about the neighbours for a quarter of an hour, oblivious to the plaintive whistle of her kettle in the kitchen telling her it was time for a nice sit-down and a cup of instant coffee.

# 10

I spent a busy day detecting – things like having my hair cut, a really long comforting chat with a nice woman in a cigar-shop, another with a bored functionary in the Labour Bureau – with full employment he had nothing to do these days. This way I was piecing bits of my puzzle together. There seemed to be nothing wrong with my disguise; I had grown more and more daring, and had penetrated such sanctums as the bureaux of the Income Tax Inspectorate, the Ministry of Social Affairs, and the adjutant of the local police force, on the pretext that I was interested in working permits recently issued for Turkish labourers in the building trade (all the Dutch labourers popped over the border to Germany every week, coming home on Friday nights with a wage packet twice the size of the one they got in Holland; a thorn in the flesh, this, of both Tax Inspectorate and Social Affairs).

Nobody, not even the adjutant, a shrewd enough chap too, guessed that I was a policeman. None of them had any real work to do, and all were delighted to find that a superior official from the Ministry of the Interior had nothing to do either, liked nothing better than a quiet natter, and had not, apparently, come here to disturb their repose. We were all friendly bureaucrats together, masonic, machiavellian, and determined that whatever we did it would take a minimum of one year to do it, because no problem is Unimportant.

But few of these folk were from Drente. Like all government officials, they were posted hither and yon at the whims of their superiors, and their opinions of Zwinderen, while illuminating, were not all that helpful. I wanted to get close to the local people, and it was just that which was so difficult. I knew, now, the silence that would fall in any haunt of the real natives if I put my nose in at the door.

I got disgusted towards the middle of the afternoon with being a functionary, and went to develop my theories in Mr Besançon's company.

'You are an expert in being a suspected stranger. Not only a foreigner but a conjuror. In other centuries you would undoubtedly have been denounced as a witch. In this century you are simply suspected of writing obscene letters.'

He smiled behind his table, where he habitually sat, I had noticed. It was a big, very solid table, ordinary softwood, put together by some local carpenter. Its legs were not turned, but rounded roughly by eye with a spoke-shave; its broad top was marked and scored by tools, hands, use, wear. A good table, and he sat there comfortably at it, as much of a king as a minister behind some pompous mahogany twirlygig in Carlton House Terrace. When he spoke, or listened, his hand passed often over the wood, much as though he got pleasure from the sturdy outlines. I liked that; I would have done the same, perhaps.

'It is largely my fault,' slowly. 'My doing, then. I avoid contact, I bury myself behind my wall, I have outlandish ways.'

'Has the wall any special significance?'

'It is an anachronism, which I accepted gratefully. A century ago, I suppose, it kept the lunatics in and deprived the public of a good stare. It still does. I lived for so long in public – I asked for nothing better. But a wish for privacy is always distrusted; seek it, and they think you wish to be rude.'

'Ha. I have noticed.'

'I do not think of it as a protection from a hostile world. It has no mental significance to me. Simply a high blind wall to keep out the curious and the prying. I admit that I sought it out, that I enjoy it. You might even say I deliberately erected it.'

'A high blind wall. Uh. Mine is not blind – a glass wall. But I can neither hear nor speak. A deaf wall.'

'It worries you.'

'Very much. You see, if I am any good at my job at all it is because as a rule I am quick to make contact with people. I talk freely to them, and tempt them into being as free with me. Then I can feel them, smell them, taste them. I'm halfway then to understanding. Without that I can never get far. This business has flummoxed policemen who know more about the local people, who are probably cleverer than me. Since I don't understand, how can I get anywhere!'

'There are any number,' said Besançon slowly, 'of things in the world – often tragic, even terrible. One does not understand, and one never will. The human being stands there helpless, at a loss, often terrified.'

'That is true.' I found myself thinking of the children with leukaemia, the clinic in Corsica; I had read about it a week or so ago in *Paris Match*. The professor in Paris said, 'Sir, your cure is worthless.' The Corsican peasants said, 'Give every child a chance.' Who was right? Both, obviously.

'Is this affair really so important?'

'Not a bit, relatively. The prevalence of road accidents is much more important. To me it is, first because it's my job to stop this kind of thing, second because I got sent here specially, told point-blank that the others had been flummoxed but that I'd better not be. I need to win this one, otherwise I'll stay a post-office counter-clerk my entire life ... It does have a certain importance all the same. Not so much in the death of two women – but an attitude of mind that is all wrong, and which I think is the underlying cause. A certain parallel with persecuting Jews.'

'This I don't follow,' said Besançon politely. I realized that I was gibbering.

'I mean that this is perhaps a small unimportant example of something we see everywhere. A mass hysteria that grows out of a mass self-deception, a mass neurosis. There is something wrong with life – blame it on a handy scapegoat. Jews, communists, negroes, Cubans – you name it, we've got it in stock. Here, so my feeling is running, there's a tendency to hate strangers. As though they were saying, "We were poor perhaps, but everything was all right till you came along." I am afraid I'm probably exaggerating this. Very likely I am. But so far, it's all I've got.'

Besançon asked, suddenly, the same question as Arlette.

'And these people who have received letters – were they strangers?'

'No idea. Don't think so, particularly. But I've no real idea, because I'm never likely to find out just who has had letters. But don't misunderstand me. It's not a real physical parallel. The letters haven't any nigger-go-home angle. Just that I get a sense of a community that is tight and closed against outsiders, and a little unimportant internal upset like this has a destructive effect that may become serious. What causes the disruption?'

'Your interest in Jews – you simply think that whatever was wrong with the Germans, they tried to make a scapegoat of the Jews?'

'I suppose that seems obvious enough; it's very broad. I couldn't narrow it much; I know nothing about Jews and precious little about Germans.'

'So you're not drawing a parallel; you're taking a vague idea as an illustration.'

'Yes.' I wondered why the point seemed so important to him. I had only brought it up, as he said, as a vaguely illustrative notion.

'Perhaps I'm making a mistake. You have only to correct me if that is so. You come to me – and you are very welcome – and you give me confidences, almost.'

'That's true. It's a way I have.'

'It wouldn't be a scheme, would it – quite a carefully arranged scheme?'

'To pretend to confide in you, as though spontaneously? With what object? To incriminate you?'

'It has been known.'

'I see that you know quite a lot about policemen.'

He smiled.

'I wouldn't be above it if I thought it necessary. Should I suspect you of something?'

'I am no judge of that. I have been suspected of so many things.'

'You are sensitive.'

'I have been interrogated by many, many policemen in my day. Perhaps now I put myself as it were automatically in the position of suspect.'

'I came, quite frankly, finding somebody intelligent, to pick his brains.'

He smiled again. 'What I have is at your disposal.'

I changed the subject. There was no use in pursuing it.


# 11


Arlette, when I got home, was looking out for me. She had taken my instructions, my silly plan, very seriously, and had filled four pages of one of my scratch pads with pure ethnographic research, quite trivial and absurd, and probably very valuable. I could turn it all over to a sociologist from the University of Yale who was making a survey of provincial towns. Like the man who wrote the absorbing book about the status seekers. I read it all carefully. She stood like a self-conscious schoolgirl having her essay corrected.

'One thing happened that was a little odd. I didn't know how to put it down briefly; I thought I could tell you if you were interested; you can judge for yourself. I'm probably imagining things straight away – I knew I'd be no good at this.'

'Tell me.'

'Housewives' snooping – incredible. If I lived here I'd turn into a window-peeper too.' She was indignant with herself.

'Tell me, then.'

'It's nothing really, and in Amsterdam I would have paid no heed at all, if I'd even noticed, which I probably wouldn't. And I wouldn't have listened. Here I did listen – avidly.'

I had to laugh. She wasn't only indignant; she was ashamed of herself.

'Woman. Stop tantalizing. Nothing is important, but observe whatever you see with total accuracy. You never know, you may discover the long-sought cure to the common cold.'

'Well . . .' Plunge. 'A couple down the road had a fight. Three doors down opposite. That's – let's see – number ten. There's a man and his wife and they have a little girl about five; long hair tied in a bow with a ribbon.'

'I'm trying to place them in my mind.'

'He has a little beige car, sort of butty-looking.'

'I know – Fiat eleven hundred. I've got him; he's a traveller in seeds and plants and things.'

It amused her, and slightly horrified her, that I was paying attention. That I had my notebook out, and had written on top of a clean page: 'Mimosastraat. No. 10. Beige mille-cento.' She was a witness; I was taking her down. I could see that she felt this to be a bit immoral after fifteen years of being married to me.

'I've learned a good deal of miscellaneous gossip about the whole street.'

'You tell me everything in order. Continue with the row.'

'The first I heard was, I was ironing in here and heard a door slamming, front door it sounded like, and a woman's voice screaming, "Peter, Peter!" So I remembered what you told me, and flew to the window – I may say that every wife in the street did exactly the same. The auto door banged too; that was the man – Peter, I take it – getting in. She flew out after him, got into the car too just as it started, and there seemed to be a sort of struggle inside, because the auto lurched all over the street. I suppose she was hanging on to the steering wheel but I couldn't see properly' – conscientious. 'Anyway it stopped down the street, out of my sight.' She went a bit pink. 'I went to the door and looked. You did tell me.'

'You weren't the only one, I'll bet.'

'If I hadn't I'd have been the only one. But I thought myself a dirty bitch, standing there blissfully enjoying someone else's private troubles. It was a very suburban scene. I mean – here, everything seems so hidden and hushed up, and therefore everybody peeks. At home nobody looks because they don't seem ashamed – people do often have fights on the pavement, after all. When they aren't ashamed, one doesn't feel ashamed oneself. Remember Mrs Brooks the greengrocer, in her nightie, racing down the street at three in the morning screaming, "Put down that black thing" – we did so wonder what she meant.'

'Everybody looked then.'

'Only because she made such a racket she woke us up – and I did so wonder about the black thing – and because I hated Brooks; slimy thing, wanting to rape one if he as much as sold half a pound of carrots.'

'Dear Mrs Brooks – extraordinary clothes she did wear... But we're digressing. Back to Peter.'

'They'd come to a standstill and were having an argument

but I couldn't make the words out. He got out then, and made as though to walk on, but she ran after him and clung. She kept on with Peter, Peter.'

'What time was all this?'

'About three; all the housewives drinking tea. Half the men in the street are travellers, commercial reps or whatnot – one often sees them at home in the afternoons. Good: Peter sort of shrugged her off, and she went down on her knees and clutched his leg. To stop him getting away, looked like. He turned round – they were at the end of the street – and I suppose he saw a whole row of housewives staring their eyes out, and I dare say that cooled him down. Anyway he suddenly turned back towards the house. She after him, and tried to hang on again. You could see she was really in a state; didn't care who was looking. Just in front of the door of their house she started clutching again and I think suddenly he got mad because he gave her a real four-penny one. I bet she has a black eye. That snapped the tension; he just took hold of her and brought her in and shut the door. There wasn't any more. Just silly, but I did think I ought to tell you.'

'Quite right, because I'm very interested.'

'Really, or do you say that to encourage me?'

'No, really. And now tell me the answers to a few things. Do you think he was mad at her all along? I mean that he walked out because he'd come in and found her in bed with the butcher – or just that he got mad at her making a scene in the street?'

'That more, I think, because he seemed quite calm and controlled till the last moment, when he smacked her – but I could be quite wrong.'

'Did it seem as though she were trying to excuse herself for something she had done, or was supposed to have done?'

'Not really. She had a sort of begging voice – it could have been. Don't leave me, or just Don't do it – whatever it was he was wanting to do when he got in the car. Oh yes, getting in – it took her a moment to get the auto door open – she shrieked, "Don't tell it, don't tell it." I've no idea what she could have meant, though – maybe nothing; she was really hysterical.'

'Right up my street,' with appetite.

Arlette looked slightly aghast at being taken seriously.

'And I can't do a damn thing. I think I'm going to yield to a temptation I've always had. I want to get to the bottom of this. I'm going to give the police an anonymous phone call.'

'Oh, darling. That's a bit revolting – do you have to?'

'How else are we to find out? One thing – I don't think I know how to place her. What's she like? Pretty?'

'Well, she's not absolutely horrible,' said Arlette charmingly. 'About twenty-seven, maybe twenty-five. Huge feet, and seems quite flat-breasted. Sort of bony. Small foxy face, quite pretty I suppose but stupe, like the baker's girl at home; the one on the corner.'

Fairly typical Arlette description – sounded as though the woman were not bad at all. Mm, another young, pretty married woman.

'Listen. This sounds to me a good example of the faintly queer type of emotional scene that's being played around here more often than one would expect, lately. It might of course be nothing at all, but again it might be significant, and I want to find out. You continue tomorrow – pally tea-drinking.'

'Oh, that awful Mrs Tattle – you've no idea. Nosy . . . she tells as much as she asks, I'm bound to admit. I know already all about her menopause and Grandpa's hernia, her daughter's boy-friend, what stars she's born under . . .'

'Lovely. Important that she doesn't think you toffee-nosed. Now I'm going to make my phone call. Amusing, in a sense, that I won't hear for days; I'll have to get a transcript of police interrogations from the burgomaster, sneakily.'

I didn't have to bother gazing out or peeping through a teeny teeny gap in the curtains myself to know that a police car stopped down the road an hour later. I sat cracking the joints of my huge, dry, knobbly fingers like Newman Noggs.

# 12

I had thought it comic, making a phone call in a hushed sticky voice, bringing the boys in blue pounding out. Comedy is never far away wherever Van der Valk is operating, our well-known cross-eyed detective with the two left feet. And his intoxicating, cliff-hanging certainty of always doing the wrong thing.

But I am quite good at ethnography, I thought with odious self-satisfaction. I was becoming quite an expert on Zwinderen, and especially on the Mimosa Street. I had masses of poignant information, provided by Arlette's great new friend Mrs Prins – a jewel, that woman; I had counted greatly on her – the milkman, and my new great friend, the secretary of the local Good Neighbours' Association. Wonderful fellow this, zealous for communal activities and Getting to Know One Another. With enthusiasm, he had shown an admiring Van der Valk all his schemes for social evenings, conversation groups, amateur drama classes, and a splendid notion for sending flowers to every member of the Association on their wedding anniversaries.

These Elks and Kiwanis were, in their own estimation, a great help to everyone, but they might have been surprised to discover what a help they were to me; I picked their brains with delight.

Enchanting to discover all the characters from Sinclair Lewis, flourishing here forty years after their time. Babbitt, Will Kennicott, Doctor Almus Pickerbaugh, the man who knew Coolidge – a Dutch Coolidge; there are many, and I have sometimes thought that Cal's immortal phrase, 'there exists no necessity for becoming excited', would make the ideal motto, graven in letters of bronze, outside Ministries, here in Holland.

I had a little map with all the houses of the Mimosa-straat. I looked at it and laughed. Cockeyed way of behaving. I hadn't any suspects at all; I had a little map and a notebook full of gossip. Not one single suspect, not even Besançon.

I knew what Besançon was, to me. He was my confidant, the secret adviser, the *chef de cabinet*, the power behind the sofa. Father Joseph. It is good when there is someone like this, someone connected with the business you are working on, yet somehow outside it. You can talk to these people almost with freedom, sometimes even with friendship. They have character in a mass of blank shapeless faces; their voices have individual timbre. I recall many times when they have shown me what to do. This time, I needed a person of this sort more than ever.

I had known, most of those other times, whom I had been looking for, and why. The trouble had been proving it without provoking a ghastly drama. I had always provoked the ghastly drama, having a childish liking for such things. But here I had nothing to prove. I had no theories, no hypotheses. The dramas had already happened; little tiny domestic dramas, nothing grandiose nor lurid. No headlines on this one. No spectacular interventions or interrogations.

I simply had to stay still, observe, learn. When I had learned, I would know. The author – as far as there was an author – would drop off the tree into my hand. No proving. There wouldn't be anything to prove. It would all be terribly obvious, and everyone would say, 'But how is it that we never thought of that?'

The crime – what a word – belonged to the town where it

had happened. An inevitable, inextricable consequence of a way of life. What were the problems, here, that had accompanied the laying of a thin veneer of glitter, a coating of wealthy materialism, on the old calvinist roots of a stick-in-the-mud country market town?

# Part three: 'Friendship'

# 1

I think that there is a streak of fatalism in most policemen. There come so many times when one has no very clear idea how to play one's cards. One throws them down – play them as they lie. I had a labyrinth here. To save my life I could not have said why I thought Besançon could help me penetrate it. I had nothing whatever to justify our little chats. Perhaps one tiny thing. It was doubtless out of character but I agreed with that State Recherche man. There was something queer about the old man, something hidden. Sinister? – no, that is not the word.

I've no idea what the word is.

But why should he have been, all along, Suspect Number One? The case against him was so very thin. It simply didn't exist. All the policemen, and now I added myself to that distinguished list, had stubbornly gone on thinking that even if he wasn't guilty of this, damn it, the fellow must be guilty of something. What?

They hadn't the faintest idea and no more had I.

I simply could not and would not believe that he had written those letters. I knew them by heart now. I could quote them from memory. They were sexy, mm; yes, but only vaguely, almost inconsequently, as though the writer had obeyed a conventional feeling that an anonymous letter has to be a bit sexy or nobody will bother reading it; too dull, else.

A religious feeling was much stronger in them. Certainly, they were very calvinist. They spoke of God and the Devil in that characteristically literal, familiar, glib way. In this person's life God and the Devil were very much physically present; looming, almost tangible. Listening, urging, arguing, fighting.

And the other kind of calvinism, the Coolidge kind – Cal for President, Cal for President – an overwhelming respectability, conservatism, love of regulation and formula and bureaucracy; a mincing mutton-headed hatred of risk and innovation.

A local person, I was sure by now – or I thought I was sure – born and bred here, with a distrust, a dislike of anything that came from outside. Cities were spoken of with fear and hatred – strongholds of the Devil. An undertone of anxiety: Zwinderen was being invaded by the Devil – the witches of Salem again – and he must be fought with his own vile weapons.

There was one queer, perhaps significant fact. The men who were attacked in the letters were all strangers. The women – I hadn't checked this yet to a watertight certainty – were all local women. Local – all from this province or the borders of it. This background, this atmosphere. I thought there was an unspoken appeal in the letters to them: not to play this background false.

Nothing was watertight. Sometimes I thought that maybe ten per cent of the letters had come to light. How could I be sure about anything in them, when I probably hadn't seen more than a tiny percentage?

Was the writer a woman? There was a feminist streak, and a fear – yes, a hatred – of men. Just men. But was this a convincing argument? I know feminist men. I am feminist myself. I know a fellow who carries it a long way. He says that only women make good business men – singularly unpopular point of view in Holland. He even says he can only be friends with women. He is a nice fellow – talks too much, but so do I. He's right in a way – I can't find myself friends with him but Arlette does.

He has quite a few loose screws. A few more and he could write letters like these.

Besançon had a sort of distrust of women. I would have to see if he had any feminist views.


## 2


I ruminated over Mr Besançon's home-made bookshelves. He sat at his table, calm and gentle as always. The eyes were very bright and steady behind those dark glasses of his, whatever the vision was like.

'You have the best kind of books,' I said suddenly.

'Have I? I value them very much, but why should you approve of them?'

'I only meant the books that are read and read till the covers fall off.'

'Ah.' He smiled. 'Have you ever read the memoirs of Aimée de Coigny?' – surprisingly.

'No idea even who he is.'

'A she, but there's no earthly reason why you ever should have heard of her. She was simply a pretty, adventurous, intelligent woman who was mixed up with many interesting persons and events during the Napoleonic time, and left interesting memoirs. She draws a very attractive portrait of Talleyrand in a library, picking up books, "talking to them as though they were alive". I like that.'

'I can see that you like memoirs.'

'To my taste, the only really interesting books. Is it not a strange thing that in the eighteenth century a complete nonentity should write memoirs that are read today with pleasure, whereas today a man whose name is known to all the world writes four hundred pages of the most wearisome sawdust?'.

'Today's celebrity is tomorrow's nonentity.'

'One wishes always to be a hundred years either ahead of or behind one's own time. Nothing can be duller than the present.'

I sat down and lit a cigar. I crossed my hands peacefully upon my ample stomach. I gazed at cigar-smoke, at Besançon.

His stillness was remarkable, untouched by the nervous tremble. There was suspicion in it, the deep-seated, ever present wariness of a man who has spent years in the hands of his enemies, treated with jocularity and feline cruelty more than with crude brutality. The world to him is nothing but policemen. No wonder he prefers the eighteenth century: the century that proclaimed that freedom of thought was universal, whatever servitude one might be born to. He can never lose sight of the fact that I may begin again at any moment to persecute him. How can he stand having me in the house? I knew well enough that I was intruding. One aspect of police training – one no longer cares whether one is intruding or not.

'I am depressed,' I said. 'I'm not enjoying this job, my own thoughts, my own actions.'

I got the smile around the eyes, the slight twitch of the wide mouth. The deeply sunk facial muscles hardly moved. Interesting mouth. The lips were thin and sensitive, but that sensitivity had been held, clamped taut, for so many years that no emotion would ever again show there. The lines all around had been cut in with a chisel and mallet.

'Develop,' said the mouth. 'Amplify. You wish to exercise your thoughts – you are a boxer, and I am your punching ball.'

'The job is tedious – but that I am accustomed to. The pressure to be a pure bureaucrat is great, as always. One wishes for situations that are cut and dried. For a case out of a textbook or a detective story – cut, dried, and pigeon-holed too. Everything tidy – the bureaucrat's dream. And they never are. They are invariably untidy, sloppy, shapeless.'

'Here, too, I must peek and pry, in a way that is mean and ignoble. These people, these – to me – total foreigners, they resent me, dislike and avoid me. They are quite right. What business have I to come here disapproving of them, laughing at them, holding up their ways to ridicule? I have to do my work, and here I cannot do it without taking away their dignity, without imposing my officially approved norms on their ways, that they've had for years. I am the government, the eternal enemy. I have never felt so strongly how destructive a force that government exerts upon a small provincial settlement, a village geared to village life.'

'So you come to me for consolation? To share your solitude with another solitary? You have, unless I gravely misjudge, other motives for your visits.'

'I have, yes.'

'You see, Inspector, you suspect me. Still. Always.'

It was so, but I was not going to let him cut me with the thin, bitter edge of his amusement at it. He knew well enough that I had no grounds for suspecting him.

'No. That is not what I meant. I think that I come for your advice.'

'However dubious I am of its value, I can scarcely refuse.'

'Has it ever occurred to you – no, I have phrased this wrongly – does it ever now occur to you, as a Jew, to feel – now – sympathy with the Gestapo? Understanding, now, can you feel a certain pity? Not for what they did – for them, the men who were your captors and persecutors?'

'Perhaps. Has this some connexion with problems of yours?'

'I don't know.'

'But let us be factual. As an abstract idea, my answer would be no. In certain circumstances, under certain conditions, I have thought that I understood my captors, as you call them, very well. Even at the time I often sympathized with them. State your case.'

I wanted to get up and walk about; I was unaccountably

restless and nervous that day. But I had to oppose, I do not know why, to his stillness and watchfulness my own. I felt remarkably young and raw; I have seen that same expression of weary calm on the faces of old policemen in their last years before they got put out to grass. I last saw it in Paris, waiting for a taxi in the rush hour outside the Gare du Nord. The agent on duty had the same complete indifference, that of the man who has obeyed orders his whole life, who has seen everything. Everything.

'I am here, possessing administrative and interrogatory powers, in a defeated, occupied land. If I were a simple official here to carry out my orders from the central government openly, honestly, I might feel less uneasy. I would take refuge in my officialdom. I would be the impersonal functionary. Because I am here secretly, anonymously, I do not fit into the pattern, and I lack the security of a formal position. You find me ridiculous?'

'Not at all. It is an interesting thought.'

'These are people whose lives and ideas I find ridiculous, but I also find myself hostile. They hate and fear me. I have a dangerous tendency to despise them, and to believe that their reactionary ways must be rooted out. They are hindrances to progress and hostile to the state administration – a very little more, and I think I would find myself with the mentality of a good Party man. It occurred to me that I would even find myself in sympathy with one of these characters – basically only a policeman like myself after all – like, say, the notorious Gestapo Müller.'

'Ah – Müller.' That smile again. 'I did not really know the gentleman. I should think that he was difficult to know.'

'I should think so too,' grinning back. 'Shadowy, opaque individual.'

'I dare say I know him as well as most,' indifferently. 'I do have to admit that I found him quite a reasonable fellow – towards me. I worked as you obviously know, in his department.'

'Oh yes – I've read the long and interesting dossier on you in the archives.'

'Yes indeed. My dossier. Hm. It would not amuse me to see it; I have no doubt that it is a thick useless rubbish-bin of irrelevant facts and inaccurate conclusions.'

'Like most,' mildly.

'Indeed. No sillier, I imagine, than the dossier on General Müller.'

'That I haven't had the pleasure of seeing.'

'I don't think you need worry that there is any striking resemblance between you,' said Besançon dryly.

That made me laugh. Talking about my neuroses, as usual, had dispelled them. I felt better, which was the whole idea. I wondered vaguely about General Müller. I had been reminded of him by one of the recurrent three-line sensation items that are the pepper in the dull stew of a page of newsprint. Müller had been seen in Nicaragua or somewhere – yet again.

'I wonder whether he'll ever turn up again,' vaguely.

'Who cares?' asked Besançon.

'That is one of the surprising facts – so many people still care, and so very deeply.'

'I don't. Do you?'

'No. Nor do I think he'll ever reappear. I was just thinking of a man who of all things was a schoolmaster somewhere in the United States. On his death-bed he said, "I am Marshal Ney." There was quite a bit of evidence – handwriting and so on. Not conclusive of course.'

'And do you believe in that tale?'

'Of course not. Apart from eyewitnesses, it wasn't in Ney's character. He had a romantic streak; he wanted to be sacrificed. He could have escaped much earlier if he'd wanted – and he wasn't in the least afraid of death. Why try and run suddenly, just as it became difficult? No – romantic legend, I'm afraid.'

'I think that General Müller behaved very similarly.'

'Just that there were plenty of people who saw Ney shot. Hell, I have to go and see the burgomaster. He's a lot duller than you – you'd make a good policeman.'

'Flattered at your compliment, but the career does not greatly appeal to me, at my time of life.'

'Don't see it surrounded by a rosy glow myself,' I said at the door. 'Does it bother you that I sit here talking nonsense?'

'Not in the least. I may even end by taking an interest in your twists of conscience.'

I walked over towards the Koninginneweg, mentally rehearsing my report.


# 3

It was the wife, again, who let me in. Just as unwelcoming as the last time. Regarding me, I thought, with more than disapproval at the husband being bothered during his free evening by another importunate clown. With suspicion, I thought. Strange that, no? I had two minutes to wait and amused myself wondering about this completely trivial fact. Why should the burgomaster's wife be suspicious of a functionary from the Ministry of the Interior in The Hague? They are, after all, an integral part of her existence; she must have met dozens. And it is part of her job to be amiable to all of them. This wife, incidentally, was known as a great charmer, most skilful at being amiable to anyone that might be of help in the husband's career. Odd?

Hell, I am going round the bend. I sit an hour with Besançon, wondering why I am suspicious of him and why he is still so patently suspicious of me, and I have it on the brain. I begin imagining that this perfectly harmless woman is suspicious of me. I'll be suspecting her next. Van der Valk will now take all parts previously played by Cary Grant in Alfred Hitchcock's films. He's not as old and even better looking, and hell with the women, I considered, gazing idly at Madame's bottom disappearing into the living-room.

Burgomaster appeared, rather falsely jaunty when he saw me; it didn't sound good at all, exactly as though he hated my guts but was putting a good face on it.

'Ah, Mr van der Valk. Uh – come into the study. I am so sorry, Ansje – but the town's welfare as usual comes first.' The wife nodded sourly. Sour just because she was enjoying the husband's company? I wondered again.

Don't ever start suspecting people – every damn person you meet will act suspiciously from then on.

'Well . . . how is it progressing?'

'It isn't a job, alas, where one can mark progress – so many houses built, so many roads mended, on the little chart that hangs above the desk. Wish it were. We'll go on not knowing for a little while longer, and then, quite suddenly, we'll know. And that will be the end of it.'

'Surely you form ideas? A certain crystallization? A narrowing of fields?'

'Certainly. There's a shape that makes itself more precise little by little. But the shape of a mentality, not a person yet. Our facts aren't complete and we cannot draw conclusions.'

'That has always been the drawback. Every investigating officer has said the same.'

'More facts will turn up. Letters will go on being written, and they won't all be suppressed. We haven't had any for a little while – but we are not to conclude from that that the writer just stops. They don't give up writing. They can't: they must go on till a crisis is reached. They want to reach a crisis.'

'But we don't – it has caused quite enough trouble already.'

'We won't let it get that far. But I'd like it if a few more letters turned up.'

'If I follow you, your method has been to build up a hypothetical portrait, and when that is complete, you will search for a person to correspond? I'm not sure I follow.'

'Haven't any hypothesis,' I said woodenly; the fellow was tiresome with his phrases. 'There is a vague similarity to the method of the robot portrait, where a composite photograph is constructed from details given by witnesses. All that needs more psychological knowledge – I haven't any. We're collecting knowledge about the author. Bit by bit. By the way, sir, have you got the transcripts of the police work in the Mimosastraat yet?'

'They aren't complete but they'll be brought to me to-morrow; you'll have them directly. You think that this woman – or her husband – has had letters?'

'I think that something caused a tension, which boiled over in a street fracas. Something painful, to blind them to the public way they were behaving. Could be letters. I very much want to get hold of more. If this pair correspond to a notion I've formed, it would strengthen my – call it sense of direction. I'd like, for instance, to know whether she is a local woman – and whether he's a local man.'

'Miss Burger could find out very easily.'

'Would you be kind enough to add a note if it's not already in the file?'

'It has a bearing on your ideas?' making a note with a presentation silver pencil.

'A bearing on character. The local people have, to my eyes, strongly marked features – what one might almost call local traits.'

'Ah, the local character.' The burgomaster smiled. 'I had difficulties with it myself when I came; I felt a good deal of an outsider. I was fortunate in that my wife comes from this part of the world – she was the greatest help. Secured, so to speak, my admission – of course in any small community the outsider is regarded with suspicion.'

'To be sure.'

'Well ... to summarize ... your confidence is not diminished.'

'Confidence ...' I had to suppress a grin; it sounded as though he was asking for the loan of half-a-crown's-worth till Monday. 'Believe me, burgomaster, there's no need of it. Patience and concentration. I only wish I was forty feet tall and had a magnifying glass. If I could achieve a minutely accurate observation of everything I'd have this person for you tomorrow. Everything down to temperature of the outside air. A naturalist – Fabre studying ants.'

The burgomaster had an expression halfway between the bemused and the disapproving.

'You can't compare human beings to ants, surely.'

'Of course not, except in one sense. There's a pressure here on human beings to conform, and not conforming is a thing that's strictly forbidden in antland.'

I shouldn't have opened my great mouth, but he held his peace. By profession, training, mentality, upbringing, moral belief, he would find it difficult to sympathize with Van der Valk's little ways. But he was intelligent, painstakingly tolerant, and had great respect for ability, whether it was the Minister, Miss Burger, or even me. If I showed ability, I would be forgiven the ants.

'I only see one drawback to your exposé – if this uh, observation, patience, takes longer than you count on – what then?'

'It always does. Never never can one sit down and study a peculiar set of circumstances the way I mentioned, like the naturalist. We have to leave that to the sociologists. Time and the taxpayer who foots the bill are our big enemies, as you know yourself, burgomaster.'

'Only too true, alas.'

'Every so often, we just have to take time by the hair; do something that may be precipitate and seem ill-judged. I won't bother you any longer, burgomaster.'

'You can pick up the report tomorrow afternoon if you wish; I'll bring it home at lunch-time.'

'I'll do that. And many thanks. We're not likely to get any further deaths, you know.'

'I sincerely hope not. You know your way?'

'Yes thanks, don't bother.'

It didn't occur to me till I was out of the door to ask him something, and by then it was too late. Had he, I wondered, told his wife that I was from the Ministry, or how had he explained my evening visits? Perhaps he was a wise man and simply hadn't offered any explanations at all.

It had got colder. I had to walk back to the main road, where I had left the Volkswagen; the wind had veered into the north and had strengthened. That will break this mild weather, I thought vaguely, and perhaps will be a good omen. I hate westerly weather. The depression by the Azores that they talk learnedly about in the weather-forecasting – to me it just sounds depressing, especially when it's south of Iceland.


'What d'you want?' asked Arlette. 'Port or a glass of milk?'

'Port, please; didn't even get a thimble of sherry from the city father this time.'

'You look happier.'

'I suppose I am happier. Not bad port this; what did it cost?'

'Bit on the sugary side. Seven and nine.'

'Weather's going easterly – I feel sharpened. And that old Besançon sharpens me; he's an intelligent old man, that. I don't feel quite so wound in moist warm blankets.'

'Penetrating?'

'A tiny bit. Not enough yet. Any more developments down the road?'

'Nothing heard or seen, though I've stared dutifully through the good net curtains.'

Arlette hates net curtains; she finds it a bore having to wash them.

'Nothing more will happen, probably. Doesn't matter; I'll get the police reports tomorrow.'

'The neighbours doubtless know. They'll recognize police a mile off.'

'That's just where we're handicapped. If you see a man step out of an auto and knock at somebody's door you think nothing of it. But the neighbours say, "Aha, she's a week behind with her insurance payments." You never can catch up with a place where everybody knows everybody else.'

'Never mind; you feel sharpened.'

'Enough, I hope, to see through walls as well as the next man. What was on the television?'

'Football. One of them lay down and pretended to be hurt. Footballers get more babyish every day. The Germans are terribly excited – they've broken some record or other.'

'What record?'

'Truly, I haven't the faintest idea. Has it any importance?'

'None whatever.'

'Hell, I've let the milk boil over again.'


# 4

I drove past the burgomaster's house, up the Koninginne-weg, road favoured by the prosperous of the little town: the more thriving shopkeepers, the senior executives of the factories. A straight, broad road, as nearly settled, ripened, as could be found in the whole raw, self-conscious community. These houses – half of them anyway – had been here ten years and were just beginning to weather. The shrubs in the trim front gardens were filling out; the grass was losing its newly planted look.

At the bottom of the main street, facing the canal, there were grand houses too. All that was patrician in the village had always lived on the Willemsdijk, in tall nineteenth-century houses with gables and painted woodwork, stained-glass windows and wrought-iron work on the front door. Here had lived the burgomaster, the notary, the advocate, the doctor and the vet. One or two were still there, steeped in solid gloomy grandeur. Good wood and not much light; velvet curtains a bit musty; tiled hallways decidedly chilly; awkward cupboards and passages; cellars and ice-cold sculleries; living-rooms that were salons, well pickled in port and cigar smoke. Ten North Frederick. Nice houses. But the notary was old and his practice was slipping; the doctor was retired; the vet drank and his young partner did the work. The old men gathered still in the big old café on the corner, and played a little billiards, and gossiped. It was a provincial life left over from the thirties. After the war, the burgomaster had moved to Number One, Koninginne-weg, at the extreme other end of the village that had become a town, and the Willemsdijk had slipped. Houses had passed to insurance companies who modernized the ground floor into an office; to wholesale potato merchants and the owners of wine shops; agencies for agricultural machinery and the County Council Road Authority.

The Koninginneweg was a poor substitute. The houses were small, mean and gimcrack: stuccoed bungalows and little two-storied villas trying to look grand and only succeeding in looking expensive. Shoddy little balconies, ridiculous names in pastrycook's French, in wrought-iron script all over the front, fake-antique carriage lamps as porch lights; unnecessary pieces of teak boarding or Tyrolean fretwork to set off the assembly-line steel windows. A lot of glass, a French window at the side, a large American auto in front for the 'standing'. One only has to glance at them to know what the inside is like – a wall of rough stones set in mortar, a parquet floor – coveted status symbol in

105

Holland – central heating and Dufy prints of yachts on the stairs. Mauve tiles in the bathroom with a matching pink wash-basin and lavatory.

Will Reinders lived in one of the newest, a square ugly little two-storied house standing in the few odd square metres that is a whacking big garden in Holland, with a miniature rock-garden, goldfish-pond and plaster-dwarf-with-a-wheel-barrow. The house stood sideways-on to the road, but a picture window gawped out of the blank side wall at me; I was standing finishing a cigarette on the pavement. I could see a youngish woman tidying the living-room, and wondered how Will had organized his house-keeping. Betty had been a very houseproud woman.

I walked along a crazy-paving path and resisted the temptation to throw the cigarette-end at the dwarf. Good humour was restored by a tremendous wrought-iron scrawl saying, 'Notre sillon'.

Will himself answered the bell, a tallish, thinnish, horse-faced man with ugly irregular teeth and a nose as bumpy as a country road. He was dressed to go out – camel auto-coat, one of those sporty ones with a violent Stewart tartan lining, soft hat in *pied-de-poule* check, and a rather obnoxious scarf. A well-polished Opel Kapitan, self-consciously this-year's-model, waited for him.

I gave him the business; the card that has the polite menace in it, which he barely glanced at.

'Yes?' with a slight frown. 'I'm sorry but I'm due at the factory in five minutes.'

'It'll get on all right without you for an hour, Mr Reinders.'

'That sounds a bit peremptory; what have I to do with – I haven't been in Amsterdam in two months.'

'I will explain everything, but indoors.'

'Have you the right to insist on that?'

'I'm afraid I have.'

Reinders checked his impatience, and put on his polite

face. 'Naturally, in that case, I'll help you any way I really can.'

A scientific executive's living-room – they tend to be dull, I thought. An active, intelligent man, but with little feeling for his home. Who has deliberately put off having children, because they are a drag on the career; who gives too much energy and enthusiasm to his little radio sets and not enough to what happens after he gets home and puts his slippers on.

This room was that of a nice chap, with pleasant brown eyes and an alert face. But a room with not enough flavour, not enough identity. Not false, not pretentious – just slightly boring.

Modern expensive furniture, fairly well designed and very comfortable. Warm oiled wood and tobacco-brown upholstery. Greenish Turkey carpet, with brown, beige and ivory patterning; nice one. Very attractive standard lamp, a slim curving trunk of natural wood with four arched branches, but clashing most heartily with the table lamp, which looked like the worst sort of wedding present. Empire reproduction; one of those slinky, vaguely Egyptian women wrapped in tight overlapping palm-leaves and clutching a torch. Plain oblong coffee-table set with tesserae, and above it on the wall a flashing splashing Karel Appel in outrageous shades of scarlet. Highly entertaining but not belonging to the arrangement opposite: a wholly bluey-greeny Monet riverscape over a little writing table.

Writing table crowned with an abominable piece of porcelain that must be a tiger – painted like a tiger – but really looked more like a dachshund.

I got the idea that Betty had read in *Marie-Claire* that the really smart woman achieves a happy blend in her home of the modern and the antique.

There were plenty of books, but they had a smirk, as though the pages had never been cut. Books of someone who doesn't mind spending money, who reads reviews and buys the ones that get rave notices. He is modern and progressive, and is all for bright biography, piquant goosed history and new-wave fiction. He has them in the house and will get around to reading them just as soon as he finds a minute.

Reinders jerked a hand abruptly at a chair, sat down himself gauchely – his legs were too long – and looked about to bite his nails. He suddenly got sick of my admiring his furniture.

'What am I supposed to have done?' irritably.

'You aren't supposed to have done anything. I am inquiring into the circumstances of a series of events, one of which is your wife's death.'

'Oh no, not again.'

'I quite agree and I would have much preferred not to bother you at all. This time it's for keeps. It has been decided, in everyone's interest, to work as far as possible incognito. Means you may know who I am but you form a small select group. Happy family, like the Bluebell girls. Not even the local police know who I am; I want this to sink in. To you and everybody else I am a busybody official from some ministry or other doing sociological reconnaissance. This conversation is in complete confidence.'

'Who gets whose confidence?'

'I mean that if you tell the truth in answering possibly embarrassing questions it doesn't have to go any further, but if you tell stories I'll know. The franker you are, the less finagling you give me, the quicker it's all over.'

'I've been frank with all the other policemen and it hasn't been the faintest help to anybody.'

I gave him my faint, subtle diplomatic smile.

'I'll help you. A piece of listening apparatus, secret, very sensitive, disappeared from this house. Your boss told me that. Despite the agreement to keep an uncomfortable fact dark. You may have other little secrets – mm?'

'Well, if you know that,' rather engaging rueful grin, 'I

don't suppose I have anything left to hide. Ask your questions and I'll do my best. I can't say I welcome you, but at the same time it would, I admit, be a relief to me to see this business cleared up once and for all. It was never tackled head-on. In my experience as an engineer that is a mistake.'

'We're understanding each other – I am the original Head-On King. It's paradoxical, but the only way I can beat the hush-hush that gets handed out to me is by suddenly emerging from dark corners and being abrupt.'

'All right. Bang away.'

'Who's doing the housekeeping for you now?'

'My sister-in-law. She's a fashion photographer, but she very kindly threw a job up to come here and help me out.'

'You might even end up by marrying her,' I said with helpful kindness.

'Why?' stiff.

'Why not? It's perfectly possible.'

'I suppose you can call it that. Remotely.' He sounded uncomfortable.

'Your wife's family, then, has had no thought of blaming you for her death?'

'Certainly not,' with a snap. 'Why should they? Some thoroughly unpleasant person – I'm glad to see you're really determined to get whoever this is – wrote filthy letters to my wife and she suffered a nervous collapse. If only she'd told me . . . I was terribly busy at the time with an extremely tricky problem . . . Of course they didn't blame me. Betty was always a nervous girl – well, I won't say unbalanced, but excitable. I mean that she always tended to get over-wound up about things that were really of slight importance.'

'Like, for instance you playing with the girls in the big naughty city?'

'I'm not hypocritical about it. I haven't any mistresses or anything. Betty wasn't small-minded.'

'Her family live near here?'

'No. Groningen.'

'That where she comes from, originally?'

'Thereabouts.'

'Your sister-in-law has to stay here then? She can't go home every night. She sleeps in the house?'

'Well, yes. Natural, uh? I mean it wouldn't be logical to do anything else.'

I enjoyed these protests; I had a lever to use on Willy, if ever I needed one.

'Sleep with her yet?'

Reinders' pale skin got red as fire; easy blusher.

'Why should you think any such thing?'

'Natural, uh? I mean it wouldn't be logical to do anything else.' I couldn't get his tone quite, that real engineer's devotion to a logical consequence, but I did my best.

'Look, you're insinuating –'

'You're a nice fellow, not good-looking but the girls find you attractive. And you find them attractive. You work hard, you're an intense, concentrated kind of person, and when you want to unwind you like to have a woman around. You couldn't help making a pass at anyone handy if Betty wasn't there. But when she was there you gave her plenty of activity.'

He squirmed rather.

'You may as well be frank; it isn't in the least disgraceful. To use your words once again, it's natural – logical. You've often thought up games to play with Betty – making love in queer places, having her dress up in funny clothes, having her walk about with nothing on, tumbling her on the bathroom floor – on this sofa – in the kitchen . . .'

Poor Will, he squirmed some more, but I had him. He was one of the progressive boys, believing in honesty. He had to say yes.

'Damn it, she was my wife.'

'I find it perfectly reasonable. But did it occur to you that you might have been seen on one or another occasion?'

110

'It has, yes.'

'You get on well with the sister-in-law?'

'Look – for heaven's sake – her family's very old-fashioned and rigid about that sort of thing.'

'You're safe from me. But you take some awful risks. They're a very God-fearing crowd around here.'

'Yes. Tripe I think it.'

'You aren't religious?'

'No, I'm a humanist. Of course I respect other people's points of view. And I don't exactly publicize my views, in this locality. Betty was religious – I've never held it against her.'

Quite.

'Sister moved out of the guest-room into yours?'

'No. I have a daily woman who does the rough work. Sees everything. Has the tongue of a rattlesnake – I don't dare get rid of her. We're very very careful.'

'Yet the person who writes letters gets to know things.'

'I've thought of that too.'

'I dare say you needn't worry over much. Your wife's suicide wasn't intended, and would have the effect of scaring our friend off your private life.'

'I've thought about it,' viciously. 'Some bastard, jealous, wanting to sleep with her himself. I know you're right and I'm a bit too fond of girls; I blame myself too for not keeping more of an eye on her. One of these sanctimonious, frightened, holy characters you get around here – frustrated as hell and without the guts to kiss a typist. Huh?'

'Maybe. Leave that to me; that's my job. If I get this sorted out fairly soon you'll be left in peace to marry your sister-in-law, without there being too much gossip locally.'

'I don't care a damn about the local gossip,' furiously.

'I'll leave you in peace now,' I said.

Gave him an uncomfortable quarter of an hour, I thought grinning, getting back into the Volkswagen. The trim, very modern white Opel flew up the road back towards the industry terrain like a chased cat. Mr Reinders in a good deal of a hurry to get back to the peaceful teasing intricacies of electronics and his recurrent temptation to pat his typist's behind.

I sat in my little auto and stared round me. There was nothing to stop me beginning Phase Two straight away, but it was nice out there. The sky had darkened to the bilious yellowish grey of a typical snow sky, and the snow itself was drifting peacefully earthwards in huge irregular lumps. I put a hand out and caught one; size of a marble, light and feathery as eiderdown, perfectly dry but with a slightly sticky, clinging feel like a cobweb. When I drew my hand in it just vanished, leaving no trace of moisture. Miraculous, lovely snow, making Drente beautiful.

I looked at the trees of the Koninginneweg, studying them in their new, stylized shapes. There was an old ragged plane, leaning out into the road at what looked a perilous angle. No – a plane was a summer tree, and no good in Drente anyway; they belonged in a hotter, drier, dustier landscape. But that yew there, stiff and upright. Menacing like all yews – wonderful those bony branches under the dollops of icing sugar. And that tiny Atlantic cedar in Will's ridiculous garden – pure, delicate, superb.

I got out of the car again and went back up the path, leaving footprints that looked as immortal as though this were Grauman's Chinese Theatre. I rang the bell, and paid close attention to the thermometer hanging in the dinky little porch. Zero exactly. Neither thawing nor freezing. Point of balance.

The woman opened, the woman seen through the window, now identified as Betty's sister and a lovely brand-new virgin untouched witness that no other policemen had had their great calloused, hairy, nicotine-stained paws on.

The type of blonde that used to be called fluffy. Not really pretty enough to be a barn-burner, but pleasant. Sweet. Kind. Teeny weeny bit silly. (Betty, in photographs, had not looked fluffy, but might well have been. She had been taller, thinner, and with more bone in the face.) Smile. Splendid teeth. Rather a beamy waist, but plenty of hip and bosom to make up. Solid well-shaped legs with too much foot and ankle. Simply bursting with health and energy. Eyes too tiny for a big forehead, and a huge puff of honey-blonde hair. I approved of all this, secretly thinking she'd be rather a bore in bed. Will's lookout not mine. All I meant was that surely you remember as a student playing the game of sitting on opposite sides of the bus and counting the number of beddable women who passed.

'Oh – did you leave something behind? You were just here with my brother, weren't you?'

'A little word with you if I may, Miss van Eyck.'

'Oh – you know my name. Uh, won't you come in out of the snow?'

'Only because it's my job. I'd better introduce myself; my name is Van der Valk and I'm an inspector of police. Don't be nervous or alarmed at that – nothing threatening about me. Simply to learn a little more, if I can, about your sister.'

'But . . . . surely you talked to Will just now?'

'Yes indeed. And he was most helpful. Good old Will. Be an excellent idea to marry him when all the fuss dies down. Good chap. Coming man; fine career in front of him.'

She had gone white, of course.

'Did – did Will tell you that?'

'Let's say that this is a little secret of yours I hold, because you have a little secret of mine. You don't know me, you don't know who I am, and in fact I haven't been here at all. I only wish to get from you a detail or two to add to what we know about your sister. Were you friends?'

'Oh yes, always; we went everywhere together till she married.'

'What is the age difference between you?'

'Just under two years.'

'Did she ever tell you any little secrets, after she got married?'

Another big blusher.

'I don't quite know what you mean.'

'I mean that when you saw her, as you did fairly often – mm?'

'Well, every couple of months or so maybe, no more.'

'Yes – you had a nice chat together. Just between girls, between sisters. She used to tell you all about her life.'

'Not particularly,' evasively.

I changed tack. 'Am I right in thinking you were both always a bit rebellious? The atmosphere at home – of course, you're fond of your home and your parents, but living there was a bit oppressive sometimes, I think.'

'I suppose that's true, yes.'

'And Betty married a bright young fellow. And you went away to learn fashion journalism. Was that a success? Are you good at it?'

'Not very,' with an honest grin.

'Did you have a good job?'

'No, rotten.'

'Were you really rather pleased to have this excuse for getting out of it?'

'Yes, to tell the truth, I was, really.' She gave me another beaming grin.

'I don't suppose the idea of fashion photographing was ever terribly well received at home either, was it?'

I got one of her straightforward, naïve looks for that – how on earth did I know so much about her? I was a policeman; I knew everything.

'You persisted even though it wasn't much of a success. But you're rather happy at the idea of Will marrying you. You and Betty used to have real heart-to-hearts about things. You both liked a good time, and occasionally, just to show you were emancipated a bit from the strait-laced ways at home, you both enjoyed feeling a tiny bit wicked.'

Very wide-eyed now. Uncanny. I wanted to laugh; they were such very easy guesses and she was regarding me as an absolute sorcerer.

'You knew about Betty's boy-friend, didn't you?'

'Yes,' she admitted. 'But there was nothing wrong, I promise. Betty would never have really . . .'

'Did you know about the letters?'

'No, honest. Betty just never said a word.'

I was sure she was telling the truth.

'She must have got all broody about them – if she'd only said something to someone it would have made her feel better, I'm sure.'

'I'm sure too. She didn't, unhappily. But looking back, thinking back, did she ever say anything, now that we have afterknowledge, that sounds to you now odd, queer, unlike her, that could point to anything to do with those letters?'

'No,' earnestly. 'I'm afraid I can't.'

'Never mind. Thank you, I hope I'll never worry you any more and –' I shook a heavy finger at her – 'no tales to anyone. Remember, you don't know who I am; you've never seen me. That's the only way I'll ever be able to find out who wrote horrible letters to your sister. So –'

'Honest.'

Coming out, the snow was denser still, the lumps thicker, more cotton-woolly than ever. I yielded to a childish impulse and, with my face turned upwards and my grim granite jaws wide open, I did a sort of balancing act for ten good seconds before I succeeded in catching the especially huge one on which I had set my sights and practically my heart. It was like spun sugar to eat – a great anticlimax.

# 5

'Wonderful livid light, all lurid and sinister. I've nothing particular to go out for again; I'm going to sit by the fire and spin.'

Arlette nodded but did not answer. She picked up my cigarettes and took one, snapping irritably at the lighter when it didn't work; it never will for her and I can never find out what it is she does wrong, although I am supposed to be a detective. Her face was closed and heavy; she had given herself a pugnacious double-chinned look.

'I'm making pea-soup,' abruptly.

This was good news. Arlette's pea-soup takes two days to make, but is worth waiting for. I made a vulgar noise with my mouth; she blew smoke in a loud nervous puff.

'I'll be happy when we're at home; I'm disliking all this intensely. This mean prying; this passionate interest in the footling street – the hatefulness of it. If I lived here I should start becoming just like the ghastly neighbours.'

'Look,' I said. 'This is the very first time that you've ever been involved, even remotely, in work of mine. I know it's disagreeable, but quite honestly I need your help. This is so simple I can't see it. So simple nobody's been able to see it. It bores me very much. I thought I'd be interested in this social study nonsense but really I'm not. The only thing I'm interested in here is Besançon – I'm feeling that I'm even becoming friends with him. I think that's why I can't make any headway here; I'm just not able to whip up interest. Today I had a talk to the husband, Reinders – remember the first girl that killed herself, poor little bitch? He's got her sister there, and is all set to marry her when the gossip dies down. In six months he won't notice any difference between her and the first one. It's dull, it's flat, it's petty – bah, I'm just as fed up with it as you are. It's my work, alas.'

She got an unwilling grin on her face.

'Shall we have a drink to give us courage?' I said.

'Of course. Alcohol for the machine.' She poured two. 'We're not really like the neighbours, you see – they don't drink at eleven in the morning.'

We drank, solemnly.

'Don't worry. We'll be home soon despite everything, and when you look at yourself you'll find you haven't changed. The first day you'll be fighting with the greengrocer about carrots.'

The grin was getting less unwilling; I don't know whether it was the drink or the sparkling line of chat.

'The first time I made pea-soup,' reminiscently, 'he said you didn't put carrots in pea-soup. I said of course that well, I did, and he got indignant. Said that pea-soup was a Dutch thing, by God, and he wasn't going to be told how to do it by any damned French women.' She took a big drink, obviously much cheered by the memory.

'You're probably the one that can see through this at a glance. I'll show you. Where's my notebook.'

She had to go and look at the soup first. It was moving, bubbling barely perceptibly with tiny subterranean up-heavals. She gave it a stir, regarded it with approval, moved the asbestos mat a centimetre and clanked the lid back on the pot. I knew exactly. One can hear every single damn thing in these horrible little houses. And that, I thought, is just the trouble. She sat down alongside me on the ridiculous sofa that was only just wide enough for the two of us and picked up her forgotten cigarette.

'There is a correlation between all these people, which I am still trying to work out. Look now. Here – first Betty; that's the wife of Reinders whom I saw this morning. Here's all the facts I can get about her.

'Next the minister's wife – pretty blank. He's packed up and gone far away; don't blame the poor devil – the gossip about him was poisonously malicious. The wife is still sitting

**117**

in one of these schizophrenic apathies. They're trying the usual things on her – electricity, insulin and so on – but they've no very hopeful results, yet at any rate.

'Here's the second suicide – the milk-products factory manager.

'This is an interesting one – waited some time, then brought three letters to the police. They aren't at all sure that there weren't more that haven't been shown. However, the letters then stopped abruptly, she says. If that's true it may be significant. She's the wife of the engineer who's building that big flat complex – he comes from near Rotterdam.

'And here is our new one down the road, though I won't have the police report on that till this afternoon. What I know is just facts available to everybody: he's the local sales manager for a range of imported drinks and comes from Amsterdam.

'Lastly – I'm not able to support this at all yet – I've put down the burgomaster.'

'Burgomaster?' Arlette was taken aback.

'I have a little man who is telling my stomach all the time that all is not as it should be with the burgomaster's wife. I have to go there to pick up that report this afternoon, and I intend to try a trick on her. If it doesn't come off, I think that I could manage to smooth it all over with oily talk.'

'But what have they in common with the other couples – you're talking about some correlation?'

I tried to explain. Even to me it sounded very silly.

'To start with, there's no proof that any of the allegations made in any of the letters are true at all. They all could be true, but I'm damn sure myself that most aren't true. If not all. I just don't believe that these people are the sinks of iniquity that is suggested.'

'But if they aren't,' said Arlette reasonably, 'why on earth pretend they are?'

'That is what is eating me, exactly. The supposition is and always has been that the author of these letters spied on people, possibly with glasses, possibly listening with this tiny radio there's been a ballyhoo about, and caught people out in acts of immorality. Conclusion, the attack is on immorality. Well, I've been wondering whether there really is all that much immorality. I can't, strictly speaking, find any trace of any.'

'But if there isn't, what is the attack on?'

'I just don't know,' I admitted, helplessly. 'The only thing I have to go on is that all the men are in positions of some influence, possibly even authority. Minister, two factory managers, a builder, a sales manager, even a burgomaster. And all of them are from outside – what we could call foreigners. Whereas all the wives are local women. That much is fairly clear. Where do I go from there?'

'You mean you want me to have a guess?'

'Just look at my notes and tell me if anything strikes you.'

'Mm,' dubiously. 'You know me – stupe. Still, I'll try.'

She read over my notes carefully. I poured a second drink for both of us and looked at my wife with affection. Very nice. Her hair needs washing, slightly.

'Lot about religion in your notes. All these women are big church-goers and the men not. Still, there's the minister, and the milk-factory man's a churchwarden. Can't be an attack on religion.'

'More a defence of religion, I've thought.'

'Attack on false gods? I can see that the letters are very calvinist. But the minister . . .'

'Seems he was a left-wing minister – unorthodox, even dangerously liberal, some people thought. Miss Burger tells me that when the rumours started a lot of people were rather jubilant.'

'So that a really hellfire right-wing calvinist would have attacked him?'

'Possibly. But it's very unsatisfactory,' gloomily.

'There's a feminist side, isn't there?'

'Which interests me greatly, but I can't see the point.'

'The letters are somehow sympathetic to the women and anti all men. And the men are strangers whereas the women are local. Huh?'

'It's too consistent, I think, to be pure coincidence.'

'And now you feel about the burgomaster . . . Could it be a local reaction – I get this sort of thing each day in the shops – less against authority than – than – government interference. Industrialization? – I mean that would account for Reinders, and the builder, and the sales manager, and even the milk-factory – and the burgomaster could be held responsible for a lot of it too? Anything in that?'

I sat up. 'What is it exactly that you get every day in the shops?'

'Well, one feels a strong hostility to the outsiders – they call them, or us, if you like – "the imports". But there's more. There's a hatred, almost, of all this progress. You hear all the old wives nattering. They don't like the modernity, the progress, the new shops or the flats, really. But I don't understand it – the depression here must have been cruel; they were all as poor as rats and now they've plenty. All got good jobs; no unemployment. How can they have nostalgia for the good old days?'

I started to interrupt but she wasn't finished.

'Of course they all say that this building doesn't help them a bit. They all moan that the new houses are far too dear for them and that nobody profits from the factories and the building but the imports, and that it hasn't helped them a bit. They say that despite all the new building the housing shortage is as bad as ever it's been. Even worse. Am I talking very stupidly?'

'Quite the contrary. A resentment of the outsider, plus strong conservative calvinist religion, plus distrust of government, plus an insinuation that all this attacks morality – it could all link up.'

'Now I'm not following.'

'You could say you disliked progress because it attacks religion, basic political beliefs, the whole foundation of their ethics. The government is too Catholic for their taste.'

'You're losing me altogether now.'

'Their big political party here – it's called Anti-Revolutionary. Very odd-sounding to us today, but in the nineteenth century there was great strength behind it, and here there still is. Anti-liberal, anti-Catholic. The Papists are the Scarlet Woman, the schools spread false doctrine – they were opposed to all the principles of the Revolution. To them universal education and giving Catholics the vote was disastrous – practically the Four Horsemen of the Apocalypse. Now a liberal minister would be seen as attacking them in the very sanctuary, and even the burgomaster, who is Anti-Rev himself, as well as orthodox Protestant, could be seen as the willing tool of the wicked politicians. Perhaps they see all this modernization as a corruption and a victory for the Great Beast of Rome.'

'You're exaggerating.'

'I've no idea whether I am or not.'

Arlette heaved a deep sigh and went over to the gramophone.

'Back to the eighteenth century,' she muttered, getting out her album of *Figaro*. 'This is too complicated for me.'

'They think the same, maybe,' I said, lighting a cigar. 'Before the Revolution and those horrible Frenchmen, life was much more their cup of tea.'

'What, aristocratic government?'

'Why not? Man knew his place in the world. Man and God worked together for salvation, and each man could attain grace through struggle. Whereas, with the Revolution, they lost their grip on God, and that worried them all dreadfully.' I relapsed into scribbling; Arlette heaved another deep sigh and started on the vegetables for her soup.

121

## 6

Between Act One and Act Two we had dinner – Hamburg steak, not really very eighteenth century, but nice. I fell into a sort of trance while Arlette did the washing-up. Halfway through Act Two – all the tremendous goings-on in Countess Almaviva's bedroom – I found myself just staring at the curtain of sound.

'I'm falling too deep into my theories,' I said at the end of the record. 'I'm going over to pick up that report – that, anyway, is my pretext. I don't think the report will tell me anything much, but I want a go at Madame Burgomaster. I probably won't be more than an hour or so.'

The maid opened the door; I put on the friendly open smile of men with genuine Persian rugs to sell, made just this last week in Middlesbrough-on-Tees.

'Van der Valk is my name. Ask Madame to be so good as to spare me a moment.'

'Oh, I have a packet she told me to give you if you came – I think she's busy.'

'Ask her just the same.'

The girl went off obediently, but was back directly.

'I'm afraid she can't spare the time,' in a saucy tone.

I beamed at her – I had already marched in three steps. 'Ah. Luckily I have plenty of time. I'll just wait till she's less busy – nice and warm it is here.' She wouldn't keep me waiting, I thought. She must know – or at least have a strong notion who I was. However good my alias, however cautious my behaviour had hitherto been, I couldn't nose around indefinitely without being rumbled. Not in private houses.

Still, I thought, it was time to come out of the shell a bit. As I had told the burgomaster, I couldn't just sit observing for an eternity. Neither the taxpayer nor the Procureur-Général would stand for that. Time for Van der Valk to show a little action.

Sure enough, there she came, rather white around the nose too. Full of indignation. Now what had she to get indignant about?

I had a feeling that it wasn't only indignation. Fear there too. I hadn't done anything to make her frightened.

'My husband's at his office. He gave me a report or something at lunch-time – or so he called it – to be left in your hands if you called. I see you have it; I cannot imagine why you should think it necessary to bother me further.'

She was eyeing the manila envelope in my hand as though it were the famous packet that, in fiction, is deposited in the litter basket for the blackmailer – the big wad of used tens and twenties. I put the envelope in my inner pocket – she interested me greatly.

'I think we'd better continue this conversation under four eyes only.' I motioned towards the living-room; she followed, stickily.

I had added several good examples to my collection of living-rooms since coming to Drente; I am bitten by them the way people are bitten by stamps or butterflies. This story, like many others, was a story of living-rooms, lived or unlived. Excellent example here of genus provincial grandeur; species higher functionary.

It was a big room, L-shaped, a pleasant room, bright and sparkling, and it illustrated well, I thought, the species. Coming in, formally, from the hall, it was dead and dry as the bones of Merovingian kings. Low coffee-table in front of the window, with a tall vase of desiccated pampas grass. In the place of honour on the wall, large tinted photograph: reigning monarch and consort, much bedizened with stars on the bosom, sashes and epaulettes, not a hair out of place, glazed stares and a general look of having eaten too much Christmas pudding. On the hearth, sawed birch logs that had been carefully dusted, and on either side a neat little electric radiator. Pale pastel rugs; beige, pink and almond green. Large sofa and arm-chairs upholstered in a most expensive and grandiose stuff – cut velvet, I thought; leaf green where cut and bottle green where not cut – acanthus-leaf pattern. All decorated with silvery green satin cushions plumped out like a poulterer's turkeys. All the seams of sofas, chairs and cushions were bound with silver cord, with flourishes and cloverleaf hitches and, at the four corners of the sofa, ending in resplendent silver tassels. Must have cost a year of my income and I would not even have dared sit in it in the morning-coat I hired from Moss Bros for Ascot. On the coffee-table was a presentation silver tray with a cut-glass decanter and six cut-glass whatnots designed to make the grocer's port taste like the Cockburn twenty-seven.

I hurried past all this holding my breath, noting in passing a glassed bookcase with chaste blue curtains, undoubtedly holding bound company reports and the volumes of *Punch* between 1867 and 1882.

Getting round the corner was a pleasant surprise; here the chairs were sat in, the television set looked at, there were engravings on the wall of views of The Hague, and the burgomaster had pipes in a rack. Wifey had magazines and a Japanese lacquer-work sewing-table with nests of cunning little drawers. Over the arms of chairs were little bronze ash-trays on broad leather straps, more ash-trays on the table – the ones that mustn't be used, Limoges enamel – and a vase of early daffodils. There was still a strong feeling that dogs and policemen were not permitted, but it was at least human.

I wasn't asked to sit down.

'And what, Mr van der Valk, can you have to say to me that is private – and what, I wonder, gives you the right to order me about in my house?'

'A burgomaster, Madame, is an important state function-

124

ary. No questionable interpretation can ever be put on his actions, or his family's; that is self-evident.'

'I fail to see . . . this impertinence . . .'

'If it were ever suggested – malicious tongues are never lacking – that there were some irregularity, misuse of municipal funds, anything you like – he can – he must – be able to disprove it openly and at once. Isn't it so? And of course he can; everything is on paper. His private life must also be above damaging insinuation. If anybody makes such remarks about an ordinary citizen he can be sued for slander, but suppose a whispering campaign were started, underhand, against a high functionary in public service, it would be difficult to combat. Disregard a whisper and that is seen as a tacit admission; deny it and you simply draw attention to there being, possibly, something that needs denying. A classic dilemma.'

'All very interesting. I must ask you to excuse me now.'

'His wife does all she can to help, of course. Superior functionaries sometimes get – one of the thorns on their rose-bush – anonymous, often vulgar, generally illiterate letters. Mostly abusive complaint from some rather simple person with a fancied grievance. You, now, have probably had similar experiences.'

'Oh my God,' she said.

'Luckily there are people whose job it is to help.'

I had been wondering why the woman was acting so strangely. I had even wondered for a moment whether I had accidentally stumbled on something even more interesting than another person who had had letters. She turned the tables on me rather neatly.

'Is it you who wrote?' she asked in a terrified whisper.

I was floored. I had had to pick my way, using very pompous formal phrases, ready to cover up if I saw I was going wrong. And here I had hit a bull's-eye – and been hit a smartish crack in my own bull's-eye. Van der Valk bereft of speech – extremely comic, thinking himself so clever.

'You mean you don't know who I am?'

'No – I mean I've seen you making those secretive calls on my husband.'

'You thought I was squeezing money out of him?'

'I don't know what I thought.'

'Didn't he tell you, then?'

'He said it was confidential.'

'I am an inspector of police, trying to sort out this rather nasty little affair. It is true that my identity was kept confidential, that I am supposed to be a civil servant making a survey. I have been working with your husband – that is the meaning of these private interviews that burned you. You thought I was blackmailing him...'

'He's been very worried and silent.'

'Ah. He's concerned about his administration, and his town – his folk. He's done a great deal for this place, and he cannot understand why some people, apparently, should take that amiss. You've shown him the letters?'

'I threw them all down the lavatory and I've never shown them or mentioned them. I didn't know – I thought it best to behave as though I hadn't had them.'

'What did they say?'

'That my husband and I were threatened with a dreadful scandal, that he would lose his position, that – this person – would help, could stop it all, if I did what he told me.'

'And what was it you had to do?'

'It was never put clearly. But – uh – immorality. I – I knew he must be not – not normal.'

'You know – or don't you? – that there have been other letters?'

'Some of the suggestions – I have been at my wits' end with worry. My husband has never mentioned it, but I have heard rumours that there have been other letters of this kind. I have even heard it said that that was why Mrs Reinders killed herself – she was supposed to have taken an accidental overdose of sleeping pills.'

126

'You knew her?'

'Not personally. I've met her – oh, I'm terribly sorry; please do sit down – at various functions and parties. She was quite a pleasant woman, a little nervous and abrupt.'

'Church functions?'

'No, I don't think so; we didn't belong to the same church.'

'You're a local woman, aren't you?'

'Well, I come from Friesland – that hardly counts as local. From the north, at least. My husband comes from Utrecht.'

'Why did you think I had written these letters?'

'But how did you know I had had any?'

'I didn't. I guessed something of the sort. Your behaviour arrested my attention.' Delightful police language. Arresting something, even if only attention. 'You have to realize that I've been on the look-out for this kind of thing. I have to – you see, people have not admitted that they have had letters. You should have told the police.'

'Yes. I do see,' shamefaced.

'In what sort of way are the letters written?'

'Newsprint cut out and stuck on paper.'

'No, I mean the kind of language, the way of speaking.'

I didn't think she was acting. Her face was very pink still; her forehead puckered up with anxious concentration. She looked like a schoolgirl who has to answer a tricky question in front of the class. She had quite lost the glossy self-possession of the burgomaster's wife, and her countrified, innocent look was showing through.

'They sound knowing in a horrible sneaky manner, and they kind of offer to protect me, in a beastly slimy way.' She had even slipped back into the schoolgirl vocabulary.

'It's a pity you haven't kept them.'

'I wouldn't have such filthy things in my house.'

'They're sexy, are they?'

Terrific blush.

'Well, in a certain way, yes, rather.'

'What way do they sound knowing?'

'Well, saying things about my husband that nobody would know – as a sort of proof that there were other things he knew.'

'For instance?'

She looked mulish. She wasn't going to tell me.

'Details – of a conversation – a private one, between my husband and myself.'

Now what did that mean? Was that a euphemism for some bedtime chat? Or did it mean that the listening apparatus was cropping up again? That thing was a pest; I didn't like it at all.

'Did it say, "I am God; I see and hear everything." Words to that effect?' I am especially fond of the phrase 'words to that effect'. Never did so short a phrase contain so much.

'Yes.'

'I'll have to decide what I can do. I can protect both you and your husband, so don't worry. Do nothing. But keep any letters you may get. Don't tell your husband; I don't see any need to worry him. I'm here twice a week to keep him informed on my researches, so you can always get hold of me.'

'I see now.' Her face had lit up as though she were allowed to go to the circus after all. 'I thought you were somebody horrible.'

I gave my reassuring laugh; Doctor Boomph telling the wine-merchant tactfully that he hasn't got cirrhosis of the liver just yet awhile.

'Be reassured. This business will soon be sorted out.'

# 7

I drove out along the Koninginneweg towards a less upper-crust side street leading back towards the main street. The houses were here more scattered, and there were patches of waste ground. It was freezing now; the snow on the ground had been flattened into icy rinks here and there and I progressed with majestic leisure, gazing around at a Drentse landscape made beautiful.

Suddenly, on the far side of the road, I saw a familiar figure, that turned away from a high rusty iron gate between two stone pillars. Besançon, in his long overcoat with its old-fashioned look, and rubber overshoes. He hadn't seen me; he was walking away slowly, upright, firm, but using a rubber-tipped stick. A casual passer-by would not notice the trill of the degenerating nervous system.

I slowed the Volkswagen and stopped. I had not before noticed those gates. A disused cemetery, it looked like from across the road. There was a low wall, and a belt of trees. On the gates was some plaque or inscription. I got out, and walked across to see.

Yes, a cemetery. Old headstones among rank grass and overgrown bushes. Pretty neglected. The gate was locked with a chain and padlock which looked as if it had been unopened for ten years. A board inside invited interested persons to apply for the key to the municipal grave-digger, but there didn't seem to have been any interested persons for quite a while. A tiny cemetery in a little sleeping neglected plot of ground with trees all round it. Forgotten, it seemed, by everyone around here, except possibly Mr Besançon.

It was like his house in the disused corner of the asylum fields. Perhaps he just liked places like that. I sympathized; so did I.

Ah, that was it. An old Jewish cemetery. The capitals of the pillars in the gateway were inscribed with thick, deep Hebrew letters. Underneath was a dedication: 'To our fellow burghers, and to all our compatriots, who disappeared, carried away into night and fog, and who never returned. 1940–45.' On the other pillar was a consoling if slightly banal text from the Book of Proverbs.

There had been Jews here once. Were there any now, besides Besançon? No community, at least. Perhaps one or two, isolated. I could always ask Miss Burger; it was the kind of thing she knew straight off.

Strange man. Says he detests Jews, never wants to see another Jew, but that does not stop him making little pilgrimages to this spot. He feels, perhaps, his essential Jewishness more than he will admit. One does not go through the camps without knowing how deep it goes, the Jewishness.

Doubtless, if questioned, he would say it made a pleasant walk, with his slight smile, in his deep level voice that still kept a German intonation. It was a kilometre from his home, along the only street in Zwinderen that had broad quiet pavements lined with trees; it did make a pleasant walk.

I got back into the auto and sat meditating. Only man of any real interest I had met or heard of around here – was that the reason why my interest in him remained so vivid? Of course there is a lot about his existence that's remarkable. A man who has survived where millions were massacred. Survived for five years, and in the innermost centre, what is more, of the Thousand Year Reich. In close communion with the nervous intellectuals like Schellenberg, the scientist soldiers like Dornberger, the weird visionaries and mad idealists like Himmler, the half-understood, misty characters like Bormann and Müller.

I knew little enough about any of them. The innermost circle – an extraordinary mixture. A few sheer gangsters –

Kaltenbrünner – and a few who remained utterly honest, scrupulous, like Berger, the *Waffen SS* chief. It was possible, even in that circle. Himmler himself had been in many ways likeable; kind, generous – no more than amiably potty, one would have thought. What impression had it all made on a Jew, in the middle there, being cynically manipulated for who knew what obscure purposes?

Some were cold and clever, merciless executants of the horrors conceived by their fearful master. But they had known – they must have known – that he was no dreadful sorcerer, but a pathetic object, mentally deluded and physically crippled by syphilitic progressive paralysis. They had known, and they had stayed true to the bitter end.

Some, anyway. Himmler one couldn't count; he was split right down the centre. Schellenberg the Intelligence chief had played both ends against the middle, one might even say idealistically. And Müller, according anyway to shadowy and inconclusive witness, including Besançon's, had played a game with the Russians. Perhaps a double game? Perhaps a triple game? Who knew? Nobody. A Jew hadn't lived alongside people like this without learning remarkable things.

I thought, as I often had, about that perplexed phrase left on the report by the State Recherche officer. 'As though he possessed some terrible secret.' Mm, the deaths of a million Jews, and the lives of a handful of the real werewolves – there were terrible secrets there. Did Besançon believe in God? And in the Devil? Very likely, but hardly in the same manner as these people here, the calvinists, the anti-revolutionaries.

This town; village; whatever you call it. It is like Besançon. There is something different and alien overlaying centuries of history. You will get throwbacks peeping through: old beliefs and old loyalties; deep distrusts and inborn, ingrained fears, suspicions, superstitions. The peasants here were rather like Jews, come to that. They asked to be left alone, allowed to have their beliefs and practices in peace. But the government, uneasy at anything that departs from the sacred norm, never can leave them in peace. Some busybody bureaucrat would be for ever fiddling at them. The German bureaucrats had simply been unable to stop fiddling at Jews.

Even now there was a certain power in these places. They were strong in their faith and their fanaticism. In Staphorst, the stranger got his camera broken, and the wrongdoer was judged their way, according to grim rules, and given what they found in the Book, to be the God-ordained punishment. Just as in Salem, in seventeenth-century Massachusetts. The Book said, 'Thou shalt not suffer a witch to live'.

Here in Zwinderen they would like to hang witches too. And bundle the bureaucrats about their business. Unfortunately, it is no longer possible, in Holland, to bundle senior functionaries. Burgomasters, say, or inspectors of police.

# Part four: 'Knowledge'

# 1

At home the vegetables were in the pea-soup, and a smoked
sausage, and the perfume was filling the house. We would
be allowed to eat some tonight, but only tomorrow would
it reach its real glory; Arlette says it has to stand overnight
before the flavour really comes out. She fishes the bone out
then, and the piece of pickled pork. This she cuts in slices
and puts on pumpernickel with lots of mustard – sacred
accompaniment to pea-soup; it isn't just soup, it's a meal,
like a bouillabaisse. I like a calves-foot in it – I enjoy that
sticky gelatinous feel, and a soup you can really jump up
and down on – but she says a beef bone gives a better
flavour.

I gave a loud greedy sniff.

'Much too early yet,' she said reprovingly. She was
sitting on top of the fire – 'behind the stove' as the Dutch
call it – reading *Match*.

'You're not to eat biscuits either; you'll spoil your
appetite.'

On a day like this all Holland makes pea-soup. Perhaps
Besançon's housekeeper would make it for him too, and he
would sit in his little room listening to the gramophone or
reading, and perhaps he would feel something of the same
content I was feeling. He had had a wife – gone up the
chimney, one of the very first. Did the man think often of the
soup she used to make? What could it be like to have no one
left? No one at all.

I felt more bored with my problem than ever. It was so
unimportant, so downright trivial. An outcrop of peasant

superstition and puritan resentment. A kind of sabotage. Whoever the person was, it was somebody pathetic and potty. It had caused, yes, two deaths, and even that was failing to get me excited. Neither Will Reinders nor the milkman looked to me very tragic.

But it was important; it was my job, my duty, my dedicated work. But I had to keep reminding myself of that. I couldn't help it; I felt bored with it that evening. I had the report on the affair in the Mimosastraat in my pocket – damn it; I could read it just as well tomorrow. It was an evening on which in Amsterdam I would have taken Arlette to the cinema. But not in Zwinderen, where the local pleasure palace catered for rustic youths; science fiction and ten-year-old American musicals. Tonight there was a comedy, the English kind with eccentric dukes, farcical burglars, a chase in their beloved old-fashioned autos, and an elderly haughty dowager who clonked insubordinate policemen with her handbag.

'What are you doing tonight?' asked Arlette lazily.

'I was just going to ask you the same.'

'Lovely Europa Cup football. Appeals – or are you going out?'

I didn't feel in the mood, oddly; usually the Europa Cup fills me with passion.

'I might, if you can bear to do without me.'

'I'll be so excited cheering that I can do without you easily. Hup Racing Club. I'm going to yell "Foul" and "Offside" with the best of them.'

I looked for something crushing to say.

'You don't know offside from a hole in the wall.'

'The wall – lovely – where they line up like chorus girls and the other tries to get a cunning kick in over the heads.' Arlette has never seen a football match in her life and doesn't know the first thing about it, but is a total addict of television games.

'Something perverted about women watching football; all those sweaty jockstraps.'

She just looked disdainful.

The soup was wonderful; I had the greatest difficulty in not overeating.


## 2


'What it is you find of interest in a boring old man with the shakes escapes me, I confess.'

'What I find of interest in the rest of Zwinderen, I must confess escapes me.'

I was beginning by now to feel at home a little in this house; I had found the position in which to be comfortable in the creaky cane arm-chair, where to find the ash-tray, how to get the right amount of light. The old man was accustomed to solitude, not used to repeated visits – and none at all at night – but had seemed glad to see me.

He was sitting as always in the upright chair behind the desk. Heaven knew what junk shop he had found it in; enormous ugly Victorian thing of mahogany upholstered in black leather, but they had understood comfort in those days. One could sit bolt upright, back supported, at a proper level for writing, without fatigue; I have never found a modern chair that allows this. His desk lamp put light on the working top, where he wanted it, but the standard lamp lit the whole room just enough; a pleasant, affectionate gleam upon the books and the face. That extremely tough face, that had survived, like the Abbé Sieyès. He had been reading when I came in, one of his shabby books that gave such vitality to the room. I looked at it.

'Memoirs of the Baron de Marbot – heard of but never read – like so many others.'

'Remarkable enough; full of good stories. Perhaps the

only sympathetic cavalry officer there has ever been. The Napoleonic period is full of interest. But I incline more and more towards the thought that the world was more interesting before the Revolution.'

He seemed in the mood for conversation; I had never known him so forthcoming. I had been afraid that he would shut up and refuse to talk.

'More interesting, or better?' Van der Valk quite ready to rush to the defence of the Republic.

'Better if you like. People's minds were less filled with demagogue sentiments. Kings bled their subjects white building grandiose copies of Versailles and everybody found it quite natural – even approved.'

'And we are now grateful for Dresden and Darmstadt.'

'Indeed. And even the idiotic castles built by Ludwig of Bavaria. The enlightened despot is something we need. There is nothing worse than the sentimental sobbing over the common man made fashionable in the last century. I detest the common man.'

I was greatly astonished. Still, I had to keep my end up.

'But the tyrant who all too frequently takes the place of your enlightened despot can only be overthrown by revolution – by your despised common man.'

'An aristocratic conspiracy,' said Besançon calmly, 'was cheaper, easier, and did less damage. Aristocrats might feel their privileges threatened by an abuse of power, but they protected the principle of monarchy, because in doing so they protected themselves.'

'One cannot reverse history.'

'Recent history is very dull. Recent history will only become interesting in another hundred years.'

'When Hitler and Stalin are no longer emotional figures?'

'And when democracy, perhaps, is out of date.'

'I was thinking today, oddly, in connexion with my work here, that perhaps the local people here would agree with you. They have a strong conservative sentiment, opposed to nineteenth-century liberalism. Based perhaps on puritan religion, which wasn't opposed to monarchy at all.'

'Perhaps that is why I find this countryside sympathetic. The people here may be superstitious, but they are more tolerant of an elderly eccentric than your precious government. Which cannot tolerate anything but the proclamation of the universal godhead of their infernal common man.'

'You're a reactionary,' I said, grinning. 'I have been thinking that my letter-writer has – dimly – this sort of feeling. Someone who also detests the government, bureaucracy, the all-powerful authority of the common man. Perhaps you're right at that. More servitude in those days, but more individual liberty too.'

Besançon gave his slow deliberate smile.

'Am I being brought, after all, under suspicion of writing these letters?'

'I'm asking only whether you'd agree that letters of this sort might be a protest against the sort of society that's taking shape here.'

'I have no idea. I might agree that in a bureaucratic society the bureaucrat is himself a prisoner of the system and might himself grow to resent it.'

To a policeman every conversation is something of an interrogation, I was thinking. Mister Bloodhound, with an enormous red nose, tracking things. The drift of what Besançon was saying was interesting me because I had been picking vaguely at the same sort of idea. His last phrase brought me up with a start. I remembered thinking that afternoon that his thoughts and his mind must have been changed a good deal by his experiences in Germany.

'We've been talking about governments,' I said. 'For a few years you lived very close to the men at the centre of an important government. Did that confirm your ideas about these subjects, or have you only arrived at them by reading eighteenth-century memoirs?'

He shrugged indifferently.

'Are you interested in the Third Reich? I am not a political philosopher. What value has an idly-held theory of mine?'

'I'm still interested in your ideas about bureaucracy. Remember that as a policeman, I am myself the prisoner you mention.'

'The Hitler régime might provide illustrations for what I have said. I saw something, certainly, of many of those men.'

'Then let's hear.'

Besançon looked at me curiously, keeping silent for some time, thinking it over. He seemed to make his mind up.

'If it amuses you . . . I dislike talking about these episodes in my life, which have no real importance. But there, there can be no real objection now. It is history; they are all gone and finished.

'Where can I begin? Perhaps with the axiom that absolute power is supposed to corrupt absolutely. It is half true, like most proverbs. I said, I think, that I approve of aristocratic governments; perhaps I should have said that power is safest in the hands of those born to power, to rule, who have no axes to grind, no little revenges to take upon society. The Reich contained many cloudy idealists – Himmler for an instance – and many men with great force of character and intelligence, who behaved with a savagery, a vengefulness, that pointed to very personal reasons for their conduct. Witness Heidrich, or Göring. Himmler, you know – extraordinary mixture of imbecility and great acumen – detested Göring, and valued Heidrich only as a highly gifted administrator. He wished to provide Germany with an aristocracy: that was his great aim; his SS was to produce this. I can quite see his point. He became fatally entangled, of course. What chance had he, not only against blood-thirsty despots, but against the civil servants that made up the third governmental group? Who also possessed power. Too much. Far too much.'

I listened with my mouth open. Who would have believed that the old man would grow so warm?

'A bureaucrat is nothing; he serves. Enclosed in a deadening mould of formality. Unless,' slowly, 'one of them is sufficiently gifted to break out – and receives unusual opportunities of exercising great power. Then, perhaps, he is more dangerous than the other two kinds. For the civil servant, it is dangerous to do anything but serve. Nothing is so dangerous as the bureaucrat in revolt.' He broke off abruptly.

'I prefer not to discuss the subject further.'

'I saw you this afternoon, while passing on some errand, by the Jewish cemetery. I looked at it later with some interest; I hadn't known there was one here.'

'Jews are everywhere. These are dead ones – to me, at least, preferable to the live ones, with their zionism – another lot busy building a bureaucracy with their mouths.'

The expression amused me.

'I enjoy hearing you on the subject of Jews.'

'It is no longer fashionable to say so' – his voice had lost the heat with which he had spoken of the ogres of the Reich, and had its usual tone again: detached, ironic, controlled – 'but there was some truth in the accusations made against them. Aristocratic governments in earlier centuries carried, no doubt, in themselves their own destruction, but they were largely corrupted, rotted, by crowds of ghetto pawn-brokers. No wonder, then, that the Teutonic Knights dreamed of by that ass Himmler feared and detested Jews. A better reason than that Heidrich had – did you know that Heidrich had himself Jewish blood? It was alluded to quite freely after his death.'

He always says 'Jews' I thought. Is not that unusual? Even an atheist Jew, I should have thought, says 'Us'.

'You don't care for Jews, yet you make a little pilgrimage to their graves.'

He did not make the sort of excuse I had anticipated.

'It was a crime, though, to murder Jews – was it not?' he inquired, mildly.


# 3


'We won,' said Arlette proudly, when I got home, not very late. 'We scored three goals. They would have drawn, but we saved a penalty.'

'Uh,' I said, totally uninterested. I kissed her absent-mindedly, and did a double-take, coming back to sniff.

'You stink of drink.'

'Just getting into training,' comfortably, 'waiting for you to get back.'

'So I see. Smell, rather.'

'You've had nothing?' innocently.

'Two cups of tea. I've been with old Besançon.'

'Fancy that. I thought you were bored and had gone off to pick up a Drentse dancing girl.'

'I do believe you're drunk.'

'Supposing that to be so,' with dignity, 'then I'm about to get drunker.' Like a child doing a conjuring trick, she produced a bottle. 'I had that hidden at home, and brought it thinking a day would come, and this is it.'

I agreed that the day had come, and picked up the corkscrew. *Paul Olive*, said the label. *Négociant à Frontignan (Hérault)*. It was yellowish, with an enormous scent that filled the whole room. I thought with some pleasure that it would not be difficult to catch up, and forgot happily all about Jews.

'I wish,' she was saying dreamily, half an hour later, 'that I had a suspender-belt with little silver bells on.'

It wasn't till I was half asleep that I remembered that I still hadn't read the report about the couple down the road, and sniggered. Arlette had her ways of combating her dislike of being a suburban housewife in an identical row of tiny mean houses in the Mimosastraat. How many of the housewives of Zwinderen, I wondered, danced tangos in their living-rooms dressed in a suspender belt. My snigger must have been sensible if not audible because Arlette muttered sleepily.

'Shut up. In my present condition I mustn't be vibrated.'

## 4

It was the most unpleasant sort of Dutch weather, next morning. By the thermometer, not so very cold – six below zero – but not a hard, clear, bearable cold. A thick sullen mist hung on the sour landscape, and a mean little wind pierced everything but a leather coat. Never had the little living-room, with its dreary furniture belonging to nobody, seemed so uncomfortable. I settled down with my report and my notebook, annoyed with myself for not being able to take it all more seriously. Perhaps it came from not having an office to go to; I am a creature of routine.

When these affairs aren't cleared up in a day they always tend to take three weeks, I told myself. In the next breath I was telling myself that I ought to have been on top of it by now. I would be getting a reprimand for wasting public funds.

Working in this left-handed way, snooping about in a pretentious shroud of anonymity, that everybody had probably seen through by now ... What was I doing away from paperwork, from the familiar police smell of the room in the big building on the Marnixstraat, from the old-maidish natter of Mr Tak?

What am I doing away from my home?

Have to make an effort. Look, three-quarters of Holland

lives in the Mimosastraat, in one or the other provincial town, and provincial towns are the same all over Europe. Think of one of the really dreadful French towns. Meanness, nosiness, obstructionist pettiness – every bit as bad as here and probably worse.

Still, there I wouldn't find the sixteen different churches. Bigotry, yes, sex, yes, and a prudish love of secretly using four-letter words – but this calvinism?

Or the ghastly heath country south of Hamburg – they had witches there. There was a doctor in Hamburg who was an expert on witches.

Sweden – this cocktail of provincial sex and calvinist religion was common coin there, to go by what one hears.

I wished I knew more, that I was not so ignorant, so inexperienced, so damned helpless. There was nothing extraordinary about this. This little town in Drente wasn't unique.

The report was no great help. The couple down the road had committed no offence, nor even a misdemeanour. The struggle to stop the car – driving without due care and attention; twenty gulden fine. It was the fear of publicity more than the twenty gulden that had helped the police twist these people's arms a little.

There had been letters all right; claimed destroyed. (Frustrated again; I wished I could get my hands on just one letter; just one.) The usual stuff, it seemed. Husband accused of corrupting the morals of all and sundry, peddling the demon drink of course, and being free with waitresses. Wife had taken it seriously because there was some truth in it apparently, and she was a jealous woman. She had made a scene. The man had wanted to go straight to the police, and this had upset her even more. To have the police in the house . . . well, now she had them. The husband had turned on her defensively and accused her of carrying on with men herself – she had boiled over then into a galloping hysteria. Anonymous letters – they should be me, I thought. I've had dozens; one always gets a few if one's name is in the paper during an inquiry.

No, it was not conclusive; just one more straw. There was a grain of truth perhaps in the allegations – the husband was one of these self-satisfied men, conscious of having good looks and a glib tongue – but our letter-writer never seemed to care greatly whether an accusation was true or not. Perhaps they are true in his mind. But whether true or false these letters could be very effective – upon the right character.

The engineer from Rotterdam – his wife had given the letters to the police too. He didn't care about them and neither did she. On inquiry he seemed to be vaguely but generally known as a skirt-chaser, and she as respectable as all the other wives. Using my alias, I had got Miss Burger to turn up some papers relative to the flat complex, had questioned her idly, and heard a bit of gossip. Not that the woman was a gossip in the neighbourhood sense, Mrs Tattle over the garden wall – she simply knew everybody. One does, as the burgomaster's secretary in a small provincial town.

I was floundering still. What was the significance of the listening apparatus? It had disappeared all right. I had never believed that it had played any real part, though. I had said, of course, that otherwise things were unexplainable, but that had been to twist what's-his-name's arm, the owner of the factory. I hadn't believed it. All the knowledge shown by the writer was either vague gossip, surely known, in-directly, to any number of people, or quite likely invented – it couldn't be proved either true or untrue.

The only piece of evidence that sounded conclusive on that point was the remark made by the burgomaster's wife, that the letter-writer had shown knowledge of a private con-versation. Hm. I had been told in Amsterdam to be very discreet indeed. I had better go easy with the burgomaster.

Why was it that whenever the police had started inquiring,

letters had promptly ceased, information had dried up, nothing had ever got anywhere? It was as though the letter-writer had some mysterious knowledge of the police activities, and in detail too.

I had thought of this a long while ago, and made a list of the people who had known something of what was going on, and what the police were up to during the long series of dragging inquiries. I had thought that with my alias I might possibly get somewhere. But this line had petered out too.

The burgomaster himself, of course. His locum, the senior town councillor. The chief of the local police. The secretary to the town council. Miss Burger – not officially, but it was plain that she was in the know about everything. Not a very encouraging list. I had done my best with it for days, ever since I had come here in fact. Five civil servants, all efficient, all blameless, all forward in church activities and social works. Organizers of charities. All married, solidly, worthily, all with children of school age – except Burger, of course, who lived alone in a flat. Equally blameless – I had observed from a discreet distance, I had even rummaged a bit about the building and the inhabitants of the block. The flats were in a double row of three to the block – six to a common entrance, and in a block like that not many of the movements of any one are missed by the other five. Miss Burger was a devout church-goer, a pillar of the Rural Christian Woman's League, the Consumers' Bond, and the Association for Better Housing.

The locum-burgomaster was keen on Scouting and Sport. Energetic about gymnastics for schoolchildren, about jamborees and educative trips abroad to ancient Greece or whatnot. If there were any mountains in Holland he would have climbed all of them. He was the moving spirit behind the local volleyball team and the projected skating rink, and had been the promoter of the rather grand swimming-bath. His wife was a good soul; model housewife and mother, whose children were impeccably sent every fortnight to get their hair cut. Man and wife were both given to the activities of the Good Neighbours' Club, where twice a week they solemnly played bridge or listened to little lectures.

As for the municipal secretary, he was the heart and soul of the Operetta Club. Besides being quite a good amateur violinist, he played draughts.

All these people were Reformed and Anti-Revolutionary. Damn it, what could I do with people like that? Rotarians, Pickerbaughs. Philistines, yes, tedious Do-Gooders whom personally I found unsympathetic, but public-spirited, with social consciences, backbone of civic virtue.

I thought again about the striking remark Besançon had made last night. That if a bureaucrat once moved into rebellion he would be a most dangerous person. It might be true. Probably in the Reich it had been true. This, however, wasn't the Reich. This was Holland.

Odd how all roads led back to Besançon.

I was slipping into a lard-like weariness and discouragement. I wasn't a step further. And yet I was so near. Why don't I get a stroke of luck, just a tiny stroke of luck? I polar-beared up and down that box of a room. There is something still I have not seen, am too stupid to understand.

I wanted to walk, but the weather was vile. The auto was in the garage with some obscure ailment and would not be ready before evening. I didn't want a drink. Since coming here to Drente I had drunk double what I did at home. There – an aperitif if I happened to be at home – and if I happened to have the time once I did get home. The occasional bottle at night split with Arlette. At weekends, perhaps a cognac after dinner. Whereas here I was drinking two or three together at all hours. Have to stop that. Getting a bit tipsy to encourage Arlette getting tipsy, sexy, and thoroughly enjoying herself was one thing. Being on the way to becoming a sort of small-time bedroom drunk was quite another.

I put my coat on muttering and stamped out irritably. It was every bit as disagreeable out as I had been led to believe. On the way I met Arlette, cross, coming back from shopping. Usually I fetched her heavy shopping with the auto; now, of course, the nastiest day of the year was the one on which I had no auto.

Unhelpful situation. On the one hand, whole rows of worthy citizens possessing the information needed to write those letters. I couldn't see them possessing the necessary malicious imagination, quite, let alone see them creeping about peering, listening.

On the other hand, Besançon, capable of imagination, of unexpected ideas, even of actions, very likely. But even with twenty telephones and a portable X-ray how could he have known enough of all these people to write those things? If there were invention, it was cunningly interwoven with fact.

It was ridiculous, I thought, to start suspecting Besançon of anything now. All the others had suspected him, so I deliberately hadn't, out of vanity. But what was it about the old gentleman that so drew the policeman's eye? I've told myself that my eye is drawn by anyone interesting and intelligent – that is complete nonsense. The more one sees of him the more one feels that there are questions there that need answering. A sulphurous smell; a sort of mephitic air.

The State Recherche officer, a special duty man from the political police, accustomed to aliens and refugees, everything and anything peculiar, had been baffled. Had been driven to the unsatisfied, unhappy, helpless annotation on his report that had fascinated me right from the outset . . . With the best will in the world I could not see the old gentleman writing dotty letters.

What old gentleman? He was not much over sixty. Still, his hardships, his past, his illness – it had put ten or fifteen years on him.

The inspector from Assen had conducted a little experiment. He had asked Besançon, politely, to cut a page of newsprint into little lozenges such as were used for the letters. With a pair of nail-scissors, which the experts declared to be the instrument used. He had obeyed calmly, not asking questions, though he had had no idea what it was all about. Despite his shaky hands his morsels of paper had been neatly snipped, but though they looked good enough the microscope showed up a characteristic unevenness in keeping with his disease – that the original letters had not had. Analysis of these could be brought no further than a guarded hypothesis that the snipper had an orderly mind and meticulous habits. Characteristics, I thought crossly, that Besançon shares with two-thirds of Holland. The paper the letters were pasted to came from the Hema, the Dutch Woolworth, as did the paste – every family in Holland possesses a pot.

The fresh air was beginning to wake me up; I strode along like my town councillor-scoutmaster on his way to some damned hillside where he could fill his lungs with the damned healthy fresh air. But I still felt like Mr Verloc, who, Conrad said, had the air of having wallowed all day fully dressed upon a disordered bed. Van der Verloc.

The gardens of all the little houses, so trim and neat in summer, were untidy with frost-bitten leaves and messy stalks left over from autumn, with drifts and patches of frozen snow. All the housewives had religiously swept their paths and patches of pavement, and the dirty, trampled snow was piled messily in the gutters, but on the minute lawns it still lay virginally. Underneath, I thought, there will be tiny green shoots; snowdrops, crocuses. It is nearly the end of February after all; spring is on its way to Drente. The clematis and jasmine on the outside walls will be waking up; the stiff pointed buds of the rhododendrons swelling. Soon a faint tinge of green around the lilac twigs. Sap and life stirring everywhere in the barren-looking sour ground.

'Except in my stupid head,' I muttered loudly. Two

teenage girls, clinging to the same bicycle, turned their untidy scarved heads, gawped and giggled in unison. The one in front pedalled heavily, flat-footed. The one behind had her knobbly feet stuck out clumsily in thick socks. Both wore cheap helanca trousers, quilted nylon jackets, and the hideous square spectacles with heavy black plastic frames considered modishly fetching by Dutch girls. Their hair looked as though it had been cut by the same nail-scissors as the newsprint. Their gay, uncouth, innocent faces had all the experience of life one gets from listening to pop singers and watching, with giggles, the bull climb up on the cow. They went on turning round and staring all the way up the road, wobbling wildly like Mr Polly.


# 5


I plodded obstinately on, the whole length of the village, all the way to the Industry Terrain. I wanted to see Reinders. I thought it might have been a mistake to have talked to Will at home.

Generally it is a good idea. To me it seems obvious that if you talk to somebody – pretty nearly anybody – in his own living-room you stand a better chance of penetrating the things that are nearly always there to puzzle one. There are flaws in all this, of course, the biggest perhaps being that there aren't any simple explanations for anything. Often there just aren't any explanations. Another big flaw is that there are lots of people who aren't at their most natural or even at their most confident in their own living-rooms.

Willy, now – at home, had he felt himself hampered, uneasy? Yes, and not only on account of the girl there, her physical presence dusting in the next room. And not only on account of things Betty had bought and chosen, herself handled, polished, dusted. It was still Betty's house, but there was even more than that. Will had been defensive and I had been clumsy. I had struck false notes, and he had been soured as well as harried. I had to try to do a bit better.

The timekeeper at the barrier recognized me, told me in a gleeful way that the boss wasn't there today. I looked pained and pensive.

'Now who had I better see?'

'Well there's Mr Smit – he's the Production Manager.'

'No, Mr Reinders, I think; I've had the pleasure of meeting him already.' I sounded fussily self-important; I was good at this role of the Man from the Ministry.

'I'll ring through for you.'

I could hear Will himself on the wire; he had a vibrating, emphatic voice, and sounded jovial.

'What gentleman? – oh, Mr van der Valk; yes, I know. Yes, by all means. Can he find his way, or shall I send a girl?'

'I'll find it,' I said. There was a rigmarole of staircases and passages but I am, after all, a detective, which is helpful when it comes to finding Room Nine.

Nine was a sort of drawing-office, not much different from an architect's with those angled boards, and the lamps and rulers that have shoulder joints and elbow and wrist and finger joints, and make it all look so easy. Two effaced pipe-smokers were busy making dodecaphonic electronic musical notation. I hurried on scared into an office with a cross-eyed girl-typist and a bustling middle-aged efficient female who told me she was Assistant to the Director. She was cheery but not very pinchable.

At last I got to Willy, right on the inside; a big office with a big metal desk, very untidy. There was a wall of bookshelves full of the kind of stuff Mr Besançon got asked to translate. There was a round table with a large model aeroplane standing on it, a sofa against the wall with a coffee-table in front of it, and the fourth wall was window, with climbing plants and a view of Drentse hinterland. By his desk Will didn't have charts with statistics, but a blackboard, with more electronic music scribbled on it. This was freehand, without benefit of mechanical elbows, and the result reminded one of the maze puzzles in children's annuals. How will Bobby Bear get out of the witches' forest (remember there is only ONE way he can be safe)? I took a look, and decided that Bobby Bear had taken the first to the right three times too often already and was about to be bagged by an ogre.

Will was wearing a loud tweed jacket, had glasses on, ink on his fingers, and chalk on his sleeve. He would have looked the maths master at the local grammar school but for a dead filtertip cigarette he was chewing on. He followed my look.

'People enjoy reading music, I'm told – if they can read it well enough. This isn't any different.'

'And the aeroplane?'

'Oh that. I built it. We've used it for various experiments; teleguiding and so on.'

'Clay pigeon.'

'Exactly.' He seemed pleased. 'Sit down if you want.' I sat on the arm of the sofa. He leaned his backside against the desk and just looked amiable and not a bit worried.

'You do computers and things, here?'

Now he looked amused, too.

'Good god no. That's something you leave to the big boys. Only Bull does that, here in Europe, and even they look like getting swallowed by the Americans. I once built an electronic cooking stove but my wife didn't like it. Preferred old-fashioned heat. Scared her; too uncanny.' He grinned, and then stopped grinning. 'I'm glad you came. I couldn't talk about it at home. Not with Cat there. It must have looked to you as though I hadn't cared for Bet at all. And I did, you know.'

He was getting younger every minute. He was looking about nineteen now.

'She wasn't unhappy, you know. She liked it here, even. It meant a lot to her that I got this job. She got a fine new house; she was proud I had a job I enjoyed and was good at.' He stared at his blackboard. 'I know of course it wasn't enough. This is a hell of a competitive world. But how would I have guessed it would go so far? Where did the catastrophe begin?'

I said nothing. Did he think I knew, or something?

'You know, electronics is not a simple thing either. If these toys were that simple everyone could have teleguided missiles. You wish, let's say, to provide certain impulses, make an inanimate object obey various complicated rules. You cook up a system of circuits and on the board it looks foolproof. You put it together and build it into your machine on the test-bed; it works perfectly. You repeat it exactly in practice and for no reason at all that anyone can understand it goes haywire, just does illogical things. You may very well never find out why, even after months of patiently studying and checking and recalculating. It seems good, but it just doesn't work. The only thing is to just scrap it, forget the whole thing, start building again from scratch. You haven't even gained any real experience to profit from, to tell you what to avoid.'

He was looking at me now with open appeal.

'I did my best. I thought she had a good life. I didn't neglect her really: I mean I thought about it; I thought she was occupied and contented and not sexually unsatisfied or anything. I suppose I just committed the mistake of thinking people are fairly simple, compared to electronic circuits.'

'A neurologist told me once,' I said vaguely, 'that the human body makes electronics look in comparison like the first steam engine.'

Will suddenly found the dead butt in his mouth, and

tossed it angrily into the big grey metal waste-basket. 'I wouldn't know. We're told that if something goes wrong it's human error – must be human error – but you feel often enough that nothing you do makes any difference.' He sat down abruptly at his desk.

'I'm talking too much. Did you want to ask me something – or tell me something?' He lit a fresh cigarette, realized he hadn't offered me one, and held the packet out with an apologetic 'sorry'.

'No. I just wanted to see, here.'

He seemed pleased.

'But I couldn't explain, not in years.'

'I can't explain anything either. There isn't any explanation.'

'For Betty? But I blame myself.'

'So do I.'

He looked mystified, but didn't press it.

'Can't blame everything on pilot's error,' I told him. 'If the little black box doesn't function . . .'

'One of these days,' he said heavily, 'the little black box won't function, and their old bomb will poop off where they least expect it. Then we're all in the soup.'

I laughed at him, then. 'You better start believing in God,' I told him, naughtily.

'I wish I did, sometimes. Like some coffee? I haven't anything much to do this morning, to be honest.'

'Sure.' Despite my confiding character, I didn't tell him I hadn't anything to do either.

I lit a cigarette too, to be pally. Of course he wasn't responsible for her death. And of course he was, as well. But that wasn't any of my business. All the fault of the little black box.

I walked on. Perhaps semiconsciously I turned into the Koninginneweg. Here the housewives did not do menial chores like sweeping pavements, and the daily girls dodged it – wasn't their pavement; my footsteps were muffled, and creaked sometimes on snow still untrodden. I had no idea at all what to do. I passed Will Reinders' ugly little house and thought it had the same awkward innocence as the girls on the bike. I did not think there was any crime there. I reached the big house on the corner – a grand affair for this three-halfpenny town, flashing with polished brass and fresh paint. I didn't think there was any crime there, either. My road was leading me towards Besançon, inevitably. What could I do about it? In some way, there lay the key to what I was searching for.

The sagging little cottage behind its high wall and the ragged row of cypresses was older and wiser than the houses in the Queen's Street, I thought, looking through the chink in the gate. I hadn't any reason for doing so but I tinkled the bell. Placid Mrs Thing came out with her duster in her hand. She showed no curiosity at seeing me – the only one in the whole of Drente that hasn't, I thought. Or perhaps Miss Burger? – no, that is more professional discretion. I thought of questioning her and decided not to. Her deposition was on the file – what more could she have to tell me?

She smiled with friendly recognition.

'Shall I bother him? – I realize it's working hours.'

'I think he'll be glad to see you. He's shaky these last few days; can't settle to his work. He's not getting any better you know,' she added rather sadly, 'but there's nothing the doctors can do, they say.' I could see that she was fond of him.

'Is the road really going to be widened?' she asked as she shut the gate carefully behind me. 'It would be an awful pity. You can't see it at present but he's done wonders with the garden.'

'I'm pleased to see you,' said Besançon, getting up and holding out his hand. There was a spark of cordiality in the quiet controlled voice. 'Sit down then, in your usual chair.

Mrs Bakhuis will bring you coffee, I feel sure; she approves of you.'

He was not at all surprised that I kept coming.

'You can't really be pleased to see me.'

'Why not? You are agreeable company. What good would it do me to be displeased? I cannot stop you coming. You are a policeman, and despite a certain unwilling sympathy you have for me, you suspect me. You do not quite know why, but you do.'

'Perfectly true – and very silly.'

'You are an intelligent man, Mr van der Valk. Stupid people stare at me owlishly, and I know they feel resentment, perhaps hatred, at my being different from the people they are accustomed to. Whereas I see your eyes constantly on me, not rudely, but trying to understand what it is that puzzles you. Yet it is all in the dossier.' He sounded resigned, as though he knew I would never understand.

He looked very small and thin in the high-backed solid chair. He rested his hands in his lap, loosely folded together. I studied the thin grey hair, the lines in the face like axe-cuts, the sharp flicker of the very bright eyes behind the mask of dark glasses. The mouth so tightened and pulled and reined in through long years that the lips scarcely showed. As always he was carefully shaved and spotlessly neat, wearing his shabby, well-brushed jacket as though it were a full dress uniform with gold lace. Looks like Captain Dreyfus, I thought, after his epaulettes had been torn off in public. He has a lot of dignity. Now there was another one to whom suspicion had clung obstinately, quite unreasoning. Even after the rather clumsy plot had been exposed, kind and honest people had refused to abandon their conviction that he was a villain and a traitor. And even now, people are ready to believe Jews capable of anything, from cheating the tax inspector to ritual child-murder.

Am I like that too? I wondered. I have, after all, nothing, absolutely nothing, of which I can suspect this man.

'You haven't in the least a Jewish physiognomy, have you?'

'I know – or knew – Jews with blonde hair and blue eyes.'

'But we still go round thinking of Jews as round-shouldered, hook-nosed, with big moist cunning brown eyes and thick sensual mouths.'

Abruptly he changed the subject.

'How long have you been a policeman?'

It surprised me, but he had a perfect right to ask. Why not?

'Since nineteen forty-six. Straight out of the army. I was one of those dimwit idealists.' That earned me the slight, vivid smile. 'A policeman is like a doctor, I thought; he serves society. The naïveté of both these ideas . . .'

'You have acquired a professionalism, a competence – and the usual police skills. But not the real police mentality.'

'You understand me better than I do you.'

'Yet you have had a successful career, already.'

I must have looked sour. 'You have had disillusion, bitter moments?' he added.

'Certainly. But I am lucky enough to have a wife with a very strong character.'

'Ah.' I could not see enough of the expression around the eyes, behind the dark glasses. 'Tell me more about your life.'

'I am one of these characters who like the wrong things and too often the wrong people. I thought myself a fair boxer when I was a boy. Thought I was a fair boxer? I thought myself a second Cerdan. But boxing is not thought respectable here – unsuitable for a public servant. I wanted to study languages, medicine, psychology – I had an idea that these things would be a help. All stopped. I had no chance: I didn't have the money for studies, you see. I got put to studying jurisprudence – very dull. Out of sheer rage, probably, I passed my examinations to become a police-officer. Went to the school for cadet officers. Got top marks in my class. Found out later that I'd got the worst recommendation in the class too, from the instructors. I became an inspector, but I've been reprimanded a dozen times, seen my seniority clipped twice for exceeding instructions. I know that my promotion is blocked. If I hadn't been lucky, and occasionally solved a few little puzzles that had flummoxed the orthodox, I'd probably be clerking behind a desk by now. I'm here now – that will be another question of luck. If I clear this up smartly, after a lot of others have ballsed it all up, it will do me a lot of good – and if I don't, as looks extremely likely, I'll be in the dog-house for ever, probably.'

'You lack the art of pleasing your superiors.' The smile had crept back.

'I lack pretty nearly everything. And especially the right mind. A fellow junior to me – and even a little stupider – got made chief inspector a month ago.'

Besançon leaned forward on the desk and seemed rapt in some thought of his own. I looked at the books. Memoirs, history, astronomy, seventeenth- and eighteenth-century writers; books in Russian, in French, in German. Suddenly he said something astonishing.

'You will clear this up, all right. It would not surprise me if you cleared up a lot of other things too, that have for long remained obscure.'

I must have looked astonished, in a stupid way. He got up, abruptly.

'I will ask you to excuse me. I do not feel well, and I think I wish to lie down for a short time.'

At that moment the door opened. Mrs Thing – I never could remember her name – with coffee for me. Besançon smiled.

'You must not think I am chasing you away. Sit here quietly, have your coffee in peace. Here,' he picked up a book from his desk and gave it me, 'read that for a while, and fortify yourself.' The dramatic works of Corneille.

Well, I certainly could do a great deal worse. He gave me a look as he went out. 'Learn what you can,' it seemed to say. 'Conclude what you like.' He shut the bedroom door behind him with no further interest in what I did.

The coffee was too hot to drink. I walked about, staring at the bookshelves. I sat down again deliberately in his chair, at his table. I bit into a biscuit, and brushed the crumbs away. I got up again to look at the record folders, rummaged through the long row of cardboard files containing typed transcripts, and left them alone again with a wrinkled nose. Technical German and Russian – jaw-breaking jargon; a language on its own. My German is none too good at the best of times.

All German music – no Frenchmen or Russians, nothing from the romantic period. Haydn, not much Bach, surprisingly little Beethoven. No, here we have later stuff. Gluck, Weber, 'Vogelhändler', 'Schwarzwald Mädel' – operettas, by heaven. And such German operettas. Opera? No Wagner, no Mozart, no Italians. But plenty, plenty of Richard Strauss.

Remarkable.

There was nothing on the desk; no memopad, no diary. Nothing like a photograph, a present, an ornament, a souvenir anywhere in the room. The room of a man who came back walking, wearing refugee charity clothes, carrying nothing. Everything that happened before 1945 wiped clean out. Fair enough.

On the desk was a Bible in old Gothic German, printed in Leipzig in 1911, and two surprises – the memoirs of Charles de Gaulle and a biography in English of Oliver Cromwell. The one I could understand – Besançon was interested in the problems of power. And the other? Cromwell's sources of power? Cromwell's calvinist conscience?

Was it not unusual that there was no book in the whole room that had anything to do with Jews? Except Feuchtwanger's best seller of the thirties, *Jew Suss*. And that was a novel.

There was nothing here for me or that was any of a policeman's business. I went home. There was a pork chop, cooked in the oven with an onion and an apple, sage, garlic, bread-crumbs, with mashed potatoes. Good. Endive à la crème to follow. And an orange.

# 6

I took my mind away with a jolt from Besançon. He was only distracting me from my business. I went, that afternoon, for a long, long walk alone. My report to the burgomaster was due that evening. I was rather late: I had to go home and change my shoes; I had to walk up to the garage again to pick up the auto, and the buggers made me wait, of course. I thought while I was waiting, about the people who were so obviously out of place here, like Will Reinders. For a first-class mind, he was a singularly naïve man. He made it so difficult for himself. He had to put Religion Reformed, Politics Anti-Rev, on all the little forms, he had to pay lip service to all the conventions he detested, and he did such silly things.

Like me, I thought. Still, I don't have to live here.

Reinders had a better job than he would have had anywhere else. The owner had explained to me that he kept his business here because his costs were two to three per cent lower than elsewhere in Holland – and it was just this money that he could devote to research, at which Reinders was good. Poor old Will, stuck in Drente.

It will obviously never occur to him that he is in several senses responsible for his wife's death – nor that to marry the sister will hardly put an end to his problem.

I thought about the lover boy, the draughtsman who had

been given the sack. A juvenile Reinders – another boy who did not believe in governments or churches, who had thought it virtually a sacred duty, as well as the handiest expression of his revolt against convention, to make love to his boss's wife. Poor Betty, she had had a hard time. I wondered whether she'd ever got as far as sleeping with the boy. Reinders would not be a difficult subject to cocufy.

I thought about 'the imports' – the other men and women who had the responsible jobs in the local factories, who lived on the Koninginneweg, who put up with Drente because they had good jobs, but were certainly all on the alert for even better jobs, that might get them out again. None of them had had letters – had they? They were the ones most likely to bring letters to the police if they did. Their positions were secure, and independent of what Zwinderen said or thought. It was only the local women, like Betty, who had been small-town women all their lives, that cared what Zwinderen said or thought. She had tried so hard. I recalled one of Will's stories; he had talked (and how he had talked) freely once I got him going. Betty had been interested in a book that had caused a lot of stir, about incest or something. He had bought it for her in Rotterdam. She had read it pretending indifference, but he had seen, he said with intolerable self-satisfaction, that she had been much shocked. Poor Betty.

Now how to explain to the burgomaster that the nets were undoubtedly getting very narrow, but that I still had no fish? Ah, there was the auto ready at last. The mechanic gave me a long lecture about the vitals of a Volkswagen, in which I wasn't in the least interested.

In the study, papers were being sorted out, a lot of municipal bumph for next day's council meeting. I said my little piece; he seemed fairly satisfied.

'Burgomaster, I have a small but pertinent question, which I must ask you not to take amiss.'

'Ask by all means.'

'I'm aware of course that you treat municipal affairs with the utmost discretion. But I would like to know whether any unauthorized person could ever get access to any confidential memoranda.'

'Oh, I understand. Similar questions were asked by the State Recherche – they were very thorough. I don't take it amiss. In this house – I often have papers here in this room. But they are kept in this cabinet, of which I have the only key. Surely there's a note to that effect in your file?'

'There is, yes. It was, paradoxically, more the complete opposite that I was thinking of. Could any personal papers of your own – perhaps a private letter, or something concerning family affairs, your wife, for instance – ever get mixed up with any official work you might have here? So that a letter, say, got brought inadvertently to the office?'

'I've never thought about it.'

'Why should you? The security aspect is all on the other boot, so to speak.'

'It could happen – it has no importance though.'

'Can you recall any such occasions?'

'Two or three, I think. Letters get into my brief-case – people who think that by writing a personal letter to my home they will somehow get a more favourable reaction. Begging letters, mostly. Miss Burger deals with them. Occasionally a genuine personal letter has got mixed up with those, probably because it had a typewritten envelope or some such reason.'

'Has anything of the sort ever happened that bothered you – I mean some item of news or information that was really no concern of anyone bar you. Of course I realize that it would only reach Miss Burger and go no further.'

'On that account I would have no worry – she's discretion itself. I do recall once a letter that I'd picked up on my way to work and had stuffed in my pocket. It came inadvertently under her eye and caused me, I admit, some slight embarrassment. But directly she read the first lines and realized its

161

personal import she handed it straight back to me, apologizing profusely.'

'Have you any objection to telling me what was in it?'

'You're not suspecting Miss Burger, are you?'

'No no, just a cross-check.'

'Well,' he hemmed, 'it was a letter from a doctor – a medical matter – concerning only myself – I'm afraid that's all I can tell you.'

'No matter.'

'If you're concerned whether Miss Burger could have discovered your identity, I can reassure you. I have a "for my eyes only" file – the correspondence relative to your purpose here went in that.'

'That does indeed reassure me.'

'Oh, I dare say Miss Burger has a certain curiosity about your doings. But she's not only well trained – she has a very strongly developed conscience.'

'Conscience as a worker?'

'Not only conscientious – that's not so rare after all in public servants – she has a tremendous sense of right and wrong; that's what makes my trust in her considerable.'

'She's rather pretty.'

'She's not unattractive. I suppose I'm so used to her I hardly notice.'

'Odd that she hasn't married.'

'She's devoted practically her whole life to public work.'

I concluded that it would be unfair to suspect the burgomaster of pinching Miss Burger's bottom.

On my way out I saw the wife hovering. She came out on to the step with me, leaving the porch light out and almost closing the front door.

'He has no idea at all,' I said carefully. 'Just behave normally with him.'

'That's one relief, at least.'

'The thing that our author knows about your husband – was it personal only to him, or did it concern you as well?'

Her voice in the dimness was uncomfortable.

'Er – just him. Myself only indirectly – I can't tell you, I'm afraid.'

'No matter. Just one query more and I'll ask no further. Was it anything that would concern a doctor?'

'No.' That was that ruled out.

'Good night, Madame.'

And now home.


# 7


Arlette was waiting for me. I have only once seen her so pinched and tense: an occasion when I was four hours late on a night when she knew I was carrying a gun; a thing I do maybe once a year. Contrary to belief, plain-clothes policemen have ordinarily no right to carry weapons.

'But what's the matter? I'm not very late. The garage was very slow.'

She did not speak, but with a nervous shudder held out a plain white envelope.

I was delighted. Yes, delighted. Never have I been so pleased.

'Is this what I think it is?'

'Yes.'

'When did it come? And how?'

'Through the letter-box. But I don't know when. It's been dark an hour. People put things in the box all the time. Children with pamphlets from shops; bargains, advertisements; sometimes two or three together.'

'Anything else come?'

'Like I say, just pamphlets.'

'Did you keep them?'

'Why should I? I never do. You want them? In the bin in the kitchen.'

I scrabbled. Yes, the local supermarket, with a banner headline about cheap vermouth and tuppence off oatmeal, biscuits and condensed milk till Saturday. A printed postcard inviting us to write for free details of extraordinarily cheap sewing machines. A little mimeographed circular reminded us that a very superior doctor of divinity would address interested persons next Tuesday at seven p.m. Subject, 'The Ecumenical Survival'.

Mm.

The envelope was quite good quality, plain, unaddressed, had been sealed. I wondered whether it was worth while to run chemical tests on it.

'I half guessed,' said Arlette miserably. 'When I read it . . .' A violent shudder.

'It's aimed at you?' Curious, very curious – when all the other women had been local.

'As far as I can see at both of us. Venomously indiscriminate.'

I sat down in the living-room and drew the paper out slowly.

'Bring both of us a drink. Just make sure the curtains are shut properly.'

'I thought of that too,' bitterly. Fright, shock, disgust. She wasn't over it by any means; she poured two glasses of port and spilt some. However, the policeman had to come in front of the husband. Sorry, Arlette.

It was all I had wished, had longed for. And more. 'The one of you is no better than the other. Hypocrites. An official from the ministry – nosing in our affairs, looking down at us because we are plain honest people. How do you have the nerve to bring a woman with you? – I should like to see her marriage papers.

'Foreign harlot – why don't you go back to whatever brothel in Paris you came out of? The women here are decent God-fearing people. They know that God watches

164

them. God was watching you. Seeing a woman behave like that in our town.

'You call yourself a public servant. Pervert, abandoned, vicious. I have written to the ministry in The Hague to denounce you to your superiors. Holland is utterly sunk in sin. But we know here what it is we have to fight. Get out and take your prostitute with you.'

No spelling mistakes, and careful punctuation. Even a question mark had been carefully clipped and inserted. I wanted to jump about with enjoyment but I was sorry for Arlette. I gave her a broad smile.

'Very tame after a few I've had. I'm unhappy that you had to see it first – but, you know, this was all I needed.'

She drank some port and tried to grin back. 'Last night when I got silly and did idiotic tricks with my suspender belt. I got seen – my god, darling. Horrible.'

'Listen to me. This is not the usual kind of letter, but it's clearly by the same writer. This is the ordinary three-a-penny abusive kind, and a complete give-away. She just couldn't resist the temptation to take a chance, wanting to show how clever she was. It'll hang her.'

'Her?'

'That's a respectable housewife talking. Snub-nosed, corseted, popeyed, with thick wooden legs and a Sunday hat. She wears glasses and has arch supports inside her sensible laced shoes.'

It was intended to make her laugh; I was glad to see it did.

'No, seriously, this is a woman. The writer of these letters isn't a man.'

'A lesbian then? No wonder she didn't take to me.'

'I think maybe a suppressed lesbian.'

'But according to the letters . . .'

'Ach, I think that was just talk. She may have booked some unexpected successes. Lots of these women – any women – have tendencies they wouldn't ordinarily dream of indulging or even formulating in conscious ideas. Men, after all, are pretty vile, mm? Here just as much as most places.'

I drank my port with enjoyment.

'Have a look. Bursts wide open. Notice "write to the ministry". Nobody, bar one or two, knows which ministry I'm supposed to come from. The cards I've shown had no address – just a phony Institute of Studies.

'On the other hand, people I've interviewed know I'm from the police. This person knows too much and not enough. But it's not written with the head to try and mislead me; the sentiments come from the heart all right.'

'I don't quite understand.'

'Somebody who has access to knowledge, who has known all along what the police were doing, who hasn't thought of querying my identity. I came with official papers from the Ministry of the Interior. Nothing so compels a bureaucrat's utter faith as an official piece of paper.'

'A bureaucrat – somebody from the municipal offices?'

'I've always thought that listening apparatus thing all my eye. I must admit I thought the peeking didn't exist either – got caught there.'

'But you said somebody who hated government interference. A bureaucrat – that is government interference.'

'Two answers, I think. The government programme only started here with the new burgomaster; that's only five years or thereabouts. The one before was a local fellow and a complete dud. One could understand that anybody left over from the old régime might easily think that the municipality had got on perfectly well before the new brooms came.'

'I can see that might be a reason but it's hardly a motive.'

'Just what bothered me. But the other reason is something Besançon suggested. He remarked that a bureaucrat who turned against his cherished principles might become very dangerous. I thought of a judge in France some few years ago, who went round the bend and burned his own court-house down.'

I could see Arlette looking at me with a dubious eye. She was thinking, I guessed, that I too was a public servant – conscientious, even scrupulous sometimes, yet with revolutionary republican notions that have done me less than no good in the eyes of my superiors.

'Remarkable how I cannot detach Besançon from this business. Step by step, he has been inseparable from all my thinking about it.'

'Yes, yes.' Arlette was not much interested in Besançon, whom she had never seen. Whereas this business touched her, now, personally. 'I want to understand. What was it exactly he said that gave you this idea?'

'I asked him about the Hitler entourage. He distinguished between the fanatic idealists, the gangsters with simple egotistical motives, and the civil servants, who devotedly thought they were really serving the state. He suggested that if one of them were to see through it all, he would become the most unscrupulous and frightful of the lot. I can readily believe that. The ordinary ones were bad enough. Think of Eichmann – the pure civil servant.'

'You mean you thought something of the sort existed here? Far-fetched.'

'All my ideas are far-fetched,' I said ruefully. 'I just thought of a bureaucrat who went round the bend attacking the very institutions he's always worshipped. It doesn't matter how I got the idea – if the psycho boys once start, they'll make the reports, and everybody believes them no matter how far-fetched they choose to sound.'

This was a Van der Valk grievance of long standing. I have seen it so often. A policeman of years' experience comes out with something like this in court, he'd be shoved straight out to graze in the meadows, whereas some little cocksure know-all doctor-boy who's read the books is listened to in religious silence. But I had learned – I would be cute enough to fill my report with bullshit about 'Having narrowly observed the demeanour of the accused'.

'I'm going to go out after supper. I still have to secure some scrap of evidence that's tangible before I can ring the bell.'

'But supper's ready. Has been for over half an hour. That wretched letter upset me so . . .'

'Well come on then; I'm hungry and I've a lot to do. One at a time, as the lion said when he ate the explorer's wife too.'

# Part five: 'Certainty'

# 1

Prowl – big word. In a sense I was going to prowl. It was perfectly true that it is a good idea to have some proof before blowing the whistle. I hadn't any proof but I was pretty sure there would be plenty found under a search warrant. I didn't have to prowl.

Van der Valk has been told several times that he decorates things too much. True enough, I suppose. I am a creature of drama, and I like doing ridiculous dramatic things. It wouldn't do any harm to prowl, though I felt quite sure now of my bird.

I wanted to walk about and meditate too. I wanted open air and movement. This was a good excuse.

The weather was not encouraging. The snow had not lain after all; it had started thawing this afternoon. Now it was freezing again, with a thin mist, a vicious sharp wind that had backed into the north, and half-melted snow and ice blackened and rotting. I wasn't going out at night in that, not in my shiny-pants bureaucrat's suit.

I put on shapeless corduroy trousers, a high-necked sweater and a padded anorak. Heavy shoes. Also a hat I am fond of; the brim comes down all round – I look like an English politician out grouse-shooting. It is only at close quarters that I am detected and expelled from this august company; only a drunken gamekeeper after all. I hadn't a shotgun but I took my binoculars. I thought that anybody who saw me would hardly identify this rural figure with the man from the Ministry; the student of ethnography, whatever that might be.

I went out of the back door. The tiny back garden was neglected grass. Really the municipal lawn-mower would have to come and do it in summer while he was busy with the road verges.

Windows glowed at me everywhere, oblong patches of brilliant light; hardly anybody had drawn their curtains even now. They were covered with condensation from the good old-fashioned fug that had been worked up within, but peeking was a simple affair to anybody who cared to make it their hobby. Television sets turned on, tea simmering on the lamp, stove going full blast. Father deep in the local paper, Mother finishing her darning while champing on a biscuit and waiting for the Play to begin on the sacred screen, children finishing their homework. This piece, the legend would be flashed on presently, is Not Suitable for Youthful Viewers. How true.

Nobody was out at this time – it was after eight-thirty – but the juvenile delinquents. And they weren't on the streets. They would be gathered in their café in the village, the motor-bikes in an untidy heap outside and the gramophone getting with it.

I walked through the 'suburbs' of the little town. A patchwork straggle, trying to keep up with the housing shortage and never succeeding; the same picture one finds everywhere in all Dutch towns, all German and Italian and Czech and Polish and . . . Streets half-finished, the raw beginnings of a park; skeletons of flats; piles of bricks and roof-tiles lying around the muddy verges; warped wooden stringers and rusty scaffolding tubes lying about in between to be tripped over. Every now and then the reminder how much of a frontier town this still was struck sharply. Streets neat and trim and lived-in collapsed into rank moorland. There were fields of curly kale between the patches where foundations had been excavated and black square pits of earth lay half full of black water. A raw church of staring brick, no bells yet hanging in the gawky tower, was surrounded still on three sides by grazing cows.

Sensibly, the bog had been drained and landscaped at the start with dragline excavators, creating little hillocks and artificial lakes. Once these were clothed with a little greenery, they would be attractive, doubtless, but the clamour for housing was such that the plan had been patchworked, without continuity. Builders had thrown up streets where roofs were already on while the pumps were still throwing dirty water out of the foundations, the workmen lurching stickily about in gumboots, the contractors struggling vainly to keep up with the five-year plan that was to raise the population of Zwinderen to twenty thousand.

The streets were temporary affairs; zigzag courses of brick hammered in over a vaguely levelled belt of coarse rubble. Sketchily founded, half-drained, they were pitted and jagged like a moon landscape. Full, too, of greasy black puddles, sudden death to high heels and an unmerciful hammering to anything but a Land Rover or a Citroën. I was accustomed to all this by now, threading a way with automatic sidesteps where the blue or orange glare of a sparse street lamp warned one of the deepest, most treacherous pits.

Everything was still and quiet; I passed one elderly man walking his dog, and was passed in turn by one ancient bicycle, its loose back mudguard rattling on the bumps, its uncertain front light wavering drunkenly. An erratic wind, wet and cold, gusted at me from all quarters, broken into a thousand draughts at every corner; the landscape was as eerie as the middle of a forest. I stopped suddenly, alert. What was that? Who was dodging about there? Nothing and nobody – a tarpaulin over a pile of builders' material was flapping to the gusts. Frolic wind, I told myself sarcastically, Zephyr with Aurora playing; ha.

The quotation suddenly clicked into place, giving me a reference I had been groping for – a book that had made

172

some stir in the thirties. I remember it because I had picked it up off a second-hand stall in a little old-maidish Surrey town where we had been billeted in wartime; it had made an amusing change from the army. *Frolic Wind* . . .

There had been a poet who had gone for a bath in the lily-pond during a thunder shower; lovely. And three dotty old sisters, one of whom lived in a tower which she kept locked because all the walls were covered with obscene pictures she had painted. Lady Athaliah, that was it.

I leaned against a pile of bricks and fastened the binoculars on a block of flats a hundred metres off. Top corner flat; first and second windows at the northern angle. Lady Athaliah's tower? I twisted the wheel delicately and a brightly lit interior sprang into focus. Ha. I could see a head, and wanted to see more. But I was too low; even at this distance I couldn't see much of a second-floor room.

I looked about. Everything was dark and deserted where I was; nothing here finished yet – this was the programme for next spring and summer. That second-floor window, with its patch of uncurtained lemon light, looked out upon a moon landscape. No passers-by. Except me, with my little peep-glass. I crossed the road and walked into a house that had a roof but no windows and no door. I hoped there would be floors. I smelt the acrid reek of wet cement, unseasoned wood and white-lead priming paint, and groped up a little steep staircase, coming out in a cell of bare unplastered brick with a metal window-frame stuck in the middle of it. Smell was the same, enriched by the builders who had been piddling in the corner; they would. But the four metres up from street level made all the difference to my sight line; Peeping Tom had now an admirable view of the tower.

No satyrs or nymphs, alas, capering across the walls. Quite the contrary. The very ordinary, very conventional living-room of an unmarried woman living alone, who is fairly well off but frugal. No taste, plenty of neatness, tidiness, fussiness. A limp picture of sheep grazing on a moor, a few frilly ornaments, a neatly polished radio with a vase of flowers standing on a square crochet mat. The inevitable tray with painted coffee-cups and ornate biscuit-tin. A calvinist interior, bare, impersonal, dull. No books to be seen, no frivolities. She led, of course, an active life, her evenings occupied with pieties, committee-sitting, visiting newly-settled families, bringing them into the fold, enlisting them too in charitable social works.

But no committee was sitting this evening.

What on earth was Lady Athaliah wearing?

There were streaks and blurs of condensation on the window; a whole panel of the view was obscured by the potted plants ranged on the sill, but when she moved I could see down to the waist – mm, reminiscent of one of the early films of Brigitte Bardot. I moved into the corner of the window-frame, stubbed my elbow, cursed, shifted the glasses carefully, and leaned out to get a better view, oblivious to everything but that extraordinary robe affair.

Watching a person through binoculars – even if that person is simply cleaning his teeth under the kitchen tap – creates a strong emotion. You are ashamed and excited. You are afraid, too, for it is like being in the ring, watching the gloves that have hurt you and will hurt you again, watching the eyes that may or may not tell you the truth. And like looking over the sights of a rifle: look it lives and laughs, unconscious of my presence; it struts about, and one minute twitch of my finger will knock it ludicrously arse over tea-kettle into eternity and that dung-heap. With binoculars you are the submarine commander, the assassin, the preacher in the pulpit. God. As well as, always, the pornographer. A strong hot emotion.

Looking at Miss Burger through binoculars was porno less perhaps because of that ridiculous filmy *négligé* thing, that reminded one of nothing so much as a brassière

174

advertisement in a women's magazine, than because it was so sad, and anything porno is so hatefully sad.

She was very painted – her mouth and especially her eyes, and that in itself was shocking. The clean scrubbed face of a Dutch woman – and only a very few years ago only whores, in Holland, were made up – has no affinity to paint, and she had done it badly, of course, over-dramatically in colours that were far too bright. After the painted face the naked body was less shocking.

She was floating about, a cigarette in her mouth in a long holder. I wondered what she was doing. I could see no other person in the room, but her face was animated by speech; her lips moved. She looked arch and grotesquely coquette. Then I saw it was a seduction scene. A solitary seduction. I understood suddenly that in another five minutes she would be making love to herself. And I was watching her from a dark empty house with binoculars.

Something very villainous happened to me at that moment. I wanted to see her. To see her below the waist I would have to climb on the roof. There would be a builders' ladder lying about, no doubt; I was, suddenly, in a tearing hurry to hunt for it.

To get to see her below the waist I was ready to hunt for a ladder and climb on the roof, was I? Now that was laughable.

The temptation of Saint Anthony was removed suddenly by a voice. Pretty rough voice at that, and quite unsympathetic to the pornographic instincts.

'Hey,' it bellowed.

Considerably startled, the pride of the police lowered the glasses and glanced downwards. With mixed feelings, I surveyed a uniformed policeman, standing burly and menacing beside his bike. He was surveying right back, not at all with mixed feelings. Stupid of me not to realize that of course they would patrol out here as well, where naughty people often come to pinch the builders' materials.

'Caught red-handed, by god,' said the rough voice. 'Just what we've been looking for these six months.' There was a snort – as near as a country policeman will get, in Holland, to a chortle, whatever that is – of self-congratulation. I felt quite regretful that I would have to spoil the fun. I took stock of my present situation, and felt extremely foolish.

'I'll come down the stairs,' I said reasonably.

'No you don't. Have you dodge out the back and make a run for it, eh? You stay there.' To reinforce his argument he lugged his cannon into view. He didn't exactly point it at me, but it was enough to make a fairly desperate criminal, like me, realize that he meant what he said.

'Now throw the glasses, clever fellow – underhand, gently. Thanks. That's evidence, see? And now you drop down to the ground. It's not high; you won't hurt yourself. Not that I'd care if you did.'

There was no earthly use in talking. I gripped the sill meekly, swung my legs out, lowered, loosened, and did a parachutist's jump on to sodden earth. The grimy black ground stuck disagreeably to my palms, and I wiped them on the corduroy trousers. That would irritate Arlette, who would doubtless otherwise think the whole thing extremely funny. To be pinched for a peeper by the municipal constabulary!

'And now march. I'm right behind you. I need one hand to wheel my bike, but I won't hesitate to fire if you break.'

I marched. At the corner of the main road into the town a police Volkswagen van came touring past.

'Hoi,' went my guardian angel.

The van stopped and a head poked out.

'What you got there?'

'Just guess.'

'Not the one that set the builders' hut on fire?'

'Nix hut, nix fire. The sex maniac.'

'Ho.'

176

'Pinched him in the act, spying in an empty house.' He waved the binoculars triumphantly.

'Ho,' impressed. 'We'll hear all about it when we get back.'

'March,' said the angel.

I sniffed the familiar police-bureau smell with affection. This had its comic side; I was beginning to enjoy myself.

'Now,' said the duty brigadier pompously, settling a form between his elbows. 'Name? ... Christian names? ... Address? ... Profession?'

'Inspector of Police.'

'You'd better not try to be funny.'

'Have a look in my pocket,' I said reasonably, and got at once a sinking feeling – I had changed, and hadn't emptied my pockets. 'No; I've just realized I haven't my identity papers on me.'

'Haw.'

'I'm serious.' It was less funny; I had to make an effort. Really, it took Van der Valk.

'You can send the van round and ask my wife to give you the papers.'

'Why bother? You're staying here; you're for the cell.'

'Look, if I'm kidding you you'll hit me on the head with a pistol, and it does me no good. I know perfectly well you'll keep me here. But when you don't check my identity, and I'm not kidding, you'll be in trouble.'

'Police where?' – sceptical. 'Fairyland?'

'Central Recherche Amsterdam.'

'Haw. What happened then? Go for a walk in the dark and lose your way, or what?'

Anything I said would have added to the comedy, so I kept my mouth shut and gave him my big frank open grin. He looked me up and down very carefully then. I could see that he wasn't only studying me, but listening attentively to the sound of my voice. Then he reached for the mobilphone transmitter key and buzzed it.

'Jan? Whereabouts are you? ... Well, tour over to the Mimosastraat. Number twenty-five. If there's a woman there you tell her that her husband's held here, and to give you his identity papers – and they'd better be convincing. Right? ... Yes, straight away.'

There was a wait of a quarter of an hour. The brigadier doodled on the back of his form. My angel breathed heavily through his nose. Nobody stopped me smoking. We didn't have any light chat to make to one another.

I could hear the noisy motor of the minibus, a squeal of brakes, followed by exaggerated door-slamming. Arlette, possibly, had been sarcastic and they were taking it out on the auto.

There she was in person, looking determined, marching in advance of a faintly ruffled bodyguard.

'What d'you bring her for, Jan?'

'She brought us.'

'Oh.'

'I'm sure all the neighbours are delighted?' I asked, catching the pocket-book she tossed me.

'Hanging out of the windows, buzzing like a beehive.'

'Bitte sehr,' I said, presenting the desk man with my police identity card and my extra-duty authorization, signed by the Procureur-Général. He read all this, chagrin tinged with awe.

'Sorry.'

'Not your fault. I changed, forgot my pocket-book, and you saw me in peculiar circumstances.' I gave the company commander's look of stern authority, taking in, in the semicircle, four open-mouthed policemen.

'Look – sir – I'll have to ring up the inspector and tell him.'

'Yes. He'll have to know straight away. And I'll have a bit of business for him myself, I rather think.'

With no great enthusiasm, the desk man reached for his telephone.

'Case is finished,' I said to Arlette. 'I'll stay here, now I am here, because there'll be a lot of paperwork. I'll have to explain straight away to the inspector here, now, what's been going on. Got a bit out of hand. Do you mind – going back to the Mimosastraat, I mean?'

'Not a bit. I can start packing. I'll be delighted. And whatever the neighbours are thinking, it no longer bothers me.'

'Pity we haven't had a bit more of that spirit.' I fixed the car patrol, which was still a bit open-mouthed, with the glittering eye. 'These kind gentlemen will give you a lift.'


# 2

The inspector of police in Zwinderen was not pleased at being rung up and dragged away in the middle of the Play, which was exciting, with gangsters. Still less was he pleased with my invasion of his territory. Least of all with having been kept in the dark.

'I'm sorry about it too. Realize, though, that I'm under orders. Wasn't my idea, and I've never liked it either. Seems the Procureur-Général himself decided that nobody was to know except the burgomaster. Total security, because of the leak over there, see?'

'Miss Burger ... good grief! I see her pretty nearly every day.'

'That's one reason at least, and not the worst either, why nobody ever suspected her. When you were on this affair initially, she must have known everything you said, thought or did. Huh? Hardly surprising that you never found out. Who would, under those conditions?'

He nodded heavily. 'Assen hammed it up too.'

'Not to speak of the State Recherche.'

'They went on at me as though there were a hole you could drive a bus through in my organization.'

I knew that he had asked for a transfer, because a State Recherche investigation looked too much of a reflection on him. The burgomaster had talked him out of it – it was in the confidential file. I felt a good deal of sympathy with him.

'Ach,' I said, 'it can soon be finished with now. It's only ten-thirty – you could pick her up straight away. Pretty certain to find all the evidence we'll need in her flat.'

'And suppose there's nothing?'

'She'll tell. You see, I saw her; that will burn her. She won't love me – here under false pretences.' For Arlette's sake, I would keep quiet about the letter I had in my pocket. The other woman too might, possibly, be grateful to have that forgotten.

'You don't think a summons – no, I can see; has to be an arrest, and the sooner the better.' He got up and put his head out of the door.

'Haas!'

'Sir.' An oldish three-striper; solid, impressive, with a lot of jaw. He looked very quiet, good man for a disagreeable job.

'Haas, I want a woman arrested now, tonight, without noise, with tact and patience; I want the warrant executed by you.'

'Sir.'

'You'll take the little auto. Don't lose sight of her; she may do something unbalanced.'

'And if she has to dress, sir?'

'Damn it, Haas, I don't have to teach you police procedure at your time of life, do I?'

'Sir.'

I was amused; it was one of the classic problems posed for the police cadets by the instructor on 'Relations with the public'.

'You are instructed to arrest a woman suspected of being a jewel thief in her hotel room, at night. You have been warned to avoid disturbance. When asked to accompany you to the bureau, the woman refuses to dress. She threatens' – with immense relish – 'to scream, tear her nightdress, complain that you have made indecent proposals to her, bruise her face and claim that you used violence. What steps will you take?'

'But why?' the inspector said suddenly to the closed door. 'Of all people . . .'

'I suppose we might find something in her past. Childhood, upbringing, early experiences. Not police work, thank heaven.'

'I have heard, I think, that she was an orphan.'

'If she was brought up in a state orphanage that might account for a few things.'

'Psychology,' with deep distaste.

'It'll all take months, no doubt. Compulsion towards public service, resentment of governmental rigidity. Meticulous, perfectionist – neurosis. Wound up with sex and strong religious feelings. Shame and horror at lesbian inclinations, which she tries to work off in social work; only makes it worse – hell, I'm only guessing.' The inspector was a local man; I wasn't going to brush his hair the wrong way by going into my notions of the calvinist wish for isolation, independence, putting the clock back, nor my feeling that to wrestle against sin with a calvinist conscience was not the best method to cure an emotional instability.

'Burgomaster'll be upset – he thinks the world of her.'

'But only as a public servant. I guess she got sick of being a cog in the machine, and wanted someone who would think the world of her as a person. What does it matter?'

'Not to us, anyway, now we've got the criminal.'

'We've got another victim,' I corrected mildly.

# 3

Miss Burger did not make a scene with chief agent of police Haas, a man she had known all her life. But when she saw me she went into hysterical tears and used four-letter words. They hadn't found the listening gadget – she denied ever having heard of it and it remained a mystery – but they found the Bardot robe which I had seen her in, walking about playing her pathetic part. And they found an envelope with cut-up newsprint.

Everybody came to ask how I had thought of her. I had prepared my answer. She had had access to all kinds of information, I said smoothly and had developed a passion for having a finger in everything. In her spare-time activities she had met and talked with all the women who had received letters. What had made her write imaginary abuse of their husbands was none of my affair. The Protestant minister, I thought, had what had seemed to her dangerously modernist leanings. I glossed over a good deal, and did not mention the burgomaster's wife. I said I had never believed much in the creeping around at night – tried it myself, I said jocularly, and got promptly pinched by the very efficient municipal police – this greatly soothed the still-ruffled inspector. I did not say that both my wife and I had found out in a disagreeable way that she did creep about at night.

The burgomaster, rung up, was very concerned, if relieved. If, I reflected, he knew about his wife he would be more of both. Maybe she would tell him when it all leaked out.

Will would be happy that no one had said nasty things about his sister-in-law.

The director of the milk factory, freed from the accusation of being free with his great healthy shiny farm girls, would be happy.

The minister would be reinstated; they might manage to cure his wife.

And Mr Besançon would doubtless be happy, when he heard that there was no longer any need for people to walk about suspecting him of heaven knew what.

It could not have been pleasant for him, the owlish suspicions of relays of policemen, all wondering why he was a queer chap.

Of course, someone who shuns society, and is not enthusiastic about his fellow citizens of the twentieth century is asking for a bad name in Holland. Land of community activities, of jolly clubby get-togethers on the slightest pretext. Our Treasurer is this week twelve-and-a-half years married; our Secretary has for fifteen uninterrupted, productive, endless years been the very cornerstone of Municipal Sanitation.

Even I had suspected Besançon, and I still didn't know what of.

I got home at about three in the morning, my paperwork done. There would be, of course, a detailed report for Mr Sailer in Amsterdam, but that could wait till I was home. Arlette, I was glad to see, had already done the packing. Not that there was all that much. About what one would have for a holiday; a couple of weeks in beautiful unspoilt Drente.

I would have to make a courtesy call on the burgomaster, in the morning.

Who would do all the little jobs like finding accommodation for officials, now that Miss Burger was due for a rest in a clinic? Dear, dear; the municipal administration would be in an uproar, with its invaluable can-do department vanished.

# 4

'If you have a courtesy call to make,' said Arlette – she had not lit the stove and we were standing perished, clutching inadequate coffee-cups to our bosoms – 'it'll just leave me time to get the house tidy as we found it. Your Miss Burger may be round the bend – I have to admit I feel awfully sorry for the woman – but she was good at her job.'

'Too good. She must have been under tremendous tension. That need to do everything, know everything, the perfectionist urge, being meticulous in the tiniest details, is a classic pointer, or was when I went to school.'

'You mean that you're glad I'm sloppy and forget things?' said Arlette, rather meanly.

I suspected that the burgomaster had after all learned something from his wife, remembered my questions, and drawn conclusions. He was full of warm compliments, nearly fulsome. Perhaps he was just extremely delighted to see my back. He promised that his own report would go off that very day to the Minister of the Interior, who would doubtless pass it on to Mr Sailer.

'I've stolen our Secretary's girl,' with a ghost of a smile. 'But I'm afraid she'll never be a patch on Miss Burger. Her mind's too much on her boy-friend.'

'Yes,' I said grinning, unable to resist it, 'I'm all for abnormality myself.'

I walked off and left the bureaucrats hard at it, making a tiny market town in Drente into an industrial town with model garden suburbs, a place of beauty and joy to live in.

Arlette had the cases in the auto. The neighbours were taking a great interest in her movements, and Mrs Tattle at the back had bustled across with her inimitable blend of helpful nosiness. I had no doubt that the theory was that I had been sacked for misdemeanour, after being arrested by the police in disgraceful circumstances most unbefitting to a functionary of some obscure Ministry. I tried to see myself as a devoted servant of Ag and Fish, and remembered a delightful Frenchman I had once known, whose family had been in Ponts et Chaussées for five generations, and who was now a painter in Santiago, Chile.

'One last call I still want to make,' I said, crowding in behind the wheel. I am tall, and fairly broad, and was wearing a winter overcoat; in a little Volkswagen one always has that minute of thinking the zipper won't close. 'I think I should drop in on Besançon. Tell him the affair is officially closed. He stands in a peculiar position – he was number one suspect for months and I never have understood why. I've suspected him myself. And it's not just because he's odd, or a Jew. There's something sinister about the man. Perhaps you'll see it.'

'I'll be interested to see him, anyway, after hearing him spoken about so much.'

'Quite apart from business, I like him. I've found myself getting friendly with the old boy,' turning the auto into the Koninginneweg.


'This is my wife.'

'Honoured, Madame,' Besançon had his neutral, indifferent voice, but he made a formal Germanic bow and kissed her hand with politeness.

'No, thanks, we won't sit down – this is just dropping in to say good-bye.'

'Really? Your affair is untangled then?'

'It is. You won't be pestered by any more policemen, I should imagine. Certainly not by me; in Amsterdam they'll all say I've wasted enough time and I'd better get back to work smartly.'

The strange look crossed his face for an instant, the look

that I had seen the first time I met him, and told him I didn't really think he had been writing potty letters. I had thought then that it might be relief. I still thought so. I didn't know, though.

'Another eccentric elderly man like myself?'

'No, no – an over-conscientious constipated female civil servant with a calvinist conscience.'

He smiled faintly. 'I seem to recall that we touched on the point in conversation. Didn't I tell you that the born civil servant is a dangerous person?'

'You did. And I think the remark helped me more than I care to admit. I haven't exactly been a shining example of deductive or even intuitive intellectual brilliance around here.'

'You must allow me to offer you both a drink.'

'Thanks but we've a long drive ahead. I do want to say that it has been a pleasure talking to you – I can't in honesty say knowing you because I don't. It was one of the few things that gave me pleasure while I was here, and I'm very grateful.'

'You are more than kind,' formally. He looked at Arlette, who was wearing her llama jacket and looking pretty. 'I have been pleased to meet you, Madame, and regret only that it should be brief. But I am old enough not to expect pleasures.'

'That's even nicer for me than for you, because I certainly don't expect to give them.' Her accent was strong this morning.

He gave her his tired, faint smile, but something had moved him; the lines on the still, hard face altered for a second.

'You remind me of my wife, strongly.' It was only an instant; he recovered himself at once.

'I quite agree; remarkable man,' Arlette said a kilometre further.

'Very. I can't reach bottom at all with him. All sorts of depths. Even his books tell me little enough.' Arlette knows that I have a passion for the book test; I have sometimes boasted, unwisely, that I can make a character assessment from a library.

'He professes no interest in religion, but he has a Bible on his desk. He dislikes live Jews, but likes dead ones. What were the others he had there? – yes, a biography of Cromwell and the plays of Corneille. An interest in conscience? – the conflict between emotion and duty – the classical dilemma? I've no idea.'

Arlette was not interested in Corneille.

'Who is Cromwell? – the name is vaguely familiar.'

'A seventeenth-century English De Gaulle,' I said rather frivolously. 'Very interesting – the Puritan conscience at its finest. The Sword of the Lord. Submitted himself completely to God, did what God told him, and once he was satisfied he knew what God wanted – utterly immovable. Good cavalry general, and a very good politician. But rather an odd study, one might think, for a Jewish atheist watchmaker with a nervous degeneration disease after five years in the Third Reich.'

'Can't be atheist, I should think.'

'Perhaps he's become calvinist,' I said, still frivolously.

'Watch your cigarette.'

'Sorry. I have to keep both eyes on the road; it's slippery ... And no books about Jews or Jewry at all, unless you count *Jew Suss* which is only a novel, if a good one.'

'Not about Jews anyway.'

'Come. Wonderful Rabbis, fearful eighteenth-century money-lenders.'

'I only meant the man isn't really a Jew at all, hm? Pretends to be a Jew.'

'Not pretends ... decides to be a Jew.' I lapsed into silence; the road was very glidy in patches.

# 5

With a huge sigh of pleasure Arlette opened her own front door.

'Only dust. Once the stove's lit and a drink poured out, we're home.'

'Where are the plants?'

'Old Mother Counterpoint has them.' This was the old lady on the ground floor who gave piano lessons, a dear old lady. Arlette was fond of her, especially as they agreed that Samson François was the only pianist in the world who can play Debussy.

'A drink, quick.'

'There's some cognac left from Zwinderen. In the brown one with the broken lock. Careful; it's only held by the strap.'

'To Drente.'

'And may we never have to go back.'

We went to bed early. I was tired, but I lay awake a long while. Reaction, I told myself.

I went next day to the office, where a good deal of humour, intended as wit, was fired at me. My boss – that old maid Commissaris Tak – was inclined to approve of me for once.

'I'm bound to say you've wasted no excessive amount of time. You're due, in justice, some time off – mm, today's Friday. Take the weekend which is due to you anyway. I'll expect you Monday morning.'

It sounded generous, but I was due the weekend anyway. Tak is good at this trick of making a regulation sound like generosity.

'You'll have to make a report to the Palais.'

'I'll be doing that over the weekend.'

But instead of going home – if I didn't get out quick he'd

get a phone call, fly up the wall, and call me back – I sat in my office for ten minutes, brooding. My colleague was out working; I had it to myself. At the end of the ten minutes I picked up the intercom telephone that links all the offices in the headquarters building.

'Morning, Klaas.'

'Hey, you back? What's new?'

'Tell you over a beer.'

'No time today.'

'Monday maybe. I wanted to know the phone number of the Jewish bureau in Vienna.'

'You don't need it. One right here in Amsterdam. They'll phone Vienna for you if they don't happen to have what you want. Don't tell me you're mixed up with that racket?'

'I'm mixed up in all the rackets,' I said ruefully. 'What's the address?'

Doctor Eli Lazarus was a mild, fat man, who looked as though his greatest enemy were no more than the female malaria mosquito. He showed no outward signs of damage; he had a smooth unwrinkled baby face with a sad joviality about it, like an intellectual comedian. But he had lost anything up to a hundred relatives in the camps – every single person he possessed. Like Besançon, like hundreds and thousands more. Can one accuse people like that of losing their integrity, their balance, their inner peace? Who knew – it was Besançon all over again – what happened to the mentality of people who had spent years in the 'dustbin of the Reich' as Heidrich called it jokingly. Exactly like Besançon, he belonged to another world; one could not reach the depths of a man like that.

He was one of the mild, implacable, kind, reasonable monomaniacs that have sworn never to rest until the last German or Slav or just plain man accused of genocide has been brought to justice. I found it a peculiar sensation just being in his office; abominable crimes were filed here the way the employment bureau filed plumbers and salesgirls. Murder, torture, sterilization, enforced prostitution, infection with mortal disease – you name it, he'd got it.

'In a certain sense, we're near the end of our tether,' he was saying in the quiet earnest voice of a man dedicated to pre-Cambrian fossils. 'We have accounted for nearly all the persons against whom we have any hope of bringing convincing evidence. Experience has shown us that not even the Superior Court in Karlsruhe can get a conviction without witnesses. I do not mean the silent witnesses – I mean men and women that can still appear, speak, exercise the power of words – "I saw, I heard, I have felt". There were so terribly few, and now, fifteen years after . . .' He rested his big double chin on a square firm hand.

'And what remains?'

'There remains a large – painfully large – file of persons whom we know perfectly well. We know their identity, we know their quite shocking history, and we know that they sometimes, quite cynically, admit everything that we could accuse them of. But we have no juridical grip upon them. We find it impossible to bring them to trial simply for lack of the compelling evidence I have mentioned.'

'It is no longer enough to say "I accuse"?'

'It is not enough.'

'And the real higher-ups? The top few, whose names are known to the whole world? Like the one who killed himself last year in Egypt, the one who is supposed to be in Paraguay? The ones that have remained lost or hidden up till now?'

A minute smile twitched at Doctor Lazarus' big shaved jaw.

'Are you falling into the temptation of the treasure hunt, Mr van der Valk?'

'You mean the so-called secrets of the Toplitz See?'

'Not exactly, though that is as good an example as any. While the Austrian authorities were diving for those so-called treasures, we were pestered with a wasps' nest of rumour. Every well-publicized figure of those times was placed by a thousand eye-witness tales within a thousand metres of that lake. Every hoary legend got a new lease of life. Even Skorzeny, who was quietly in Spain and is in any case no criminal at all. Even Müller, hardiest and most persistent legend of all.'

'Tell me.'

'The treasure hunt, Mr van der Valk, consists largely of following up people who say they have seen Müller. It happens constantly. Only today we have a long tale that he is directing the secret police in Albania. It is and remains a chronic obsession.'

'And what do you know for certain about Müller?'

'For certain, not even if he is alive at all. We have followed innumerable false trails, some of which seemed remarkably authentic, so great is the aura, the sort of sinister romance, that surrounds Müller's name. Who – tell me – can come to me and claim he has even a remote notion what Müller looks like? There exist descriptions, photographs, you might answer. I will reply that these photographs and descriptions are of anybody and everybody. I could go here with you into the street, and in a quarter of an hour point you out twenty Müllers – a tram-conductor, a clerk at the Bourse, the teller of your bank.'

'I see.'

'We know, of course, certain facts, such as those that enabled us to examine the grave in Berlin, but we cannot say, "That is the man". And we have said, so many times, "That is not the man". Müller defeats us – on that plane. Further, there are curious inconsistencies in all the accounts, contemporary accounts you understand, of the man's actions, behaviour. To take one of the classic examples, a British officer, Captain Best, who was interrogated by Müller. He mentions the features that have become cliché – the eyes, the shouting and so on – and then remarks pleasantly, "I found him rather a decent little man." We do of course,' dryly, 'have evidence of the contrary.'

'And is there nothing to be done then?'

'We wait. As we do with many more. Evidence has been secured against people whose cases were given up as hopeless. After so many years, some of these persons have felt sufficiently secure – and, I should add, sufficiently protected – to creep out into the open. They range,' with a ferocious irony, 'from farm-labourers in Schleswig-Holstein to the directors of old people's homes.'

'I am very grateful to you, Doctor Lazarus.'

'I am quite at your disposal. Should you find, in the course of your duties – as, if I have understood the purpose of your visit, you may guess you can find – the tiniest of facts that may fit into a larger pattern, do not hesitate to apply to me. But let me warn you against becoming obsessed by the treasure hunt. There are many, many, many men, less widely known, with whom justice could be just as summary.'

'Even if you caught Müller, you could not hang him twice.'

'Just so, Inspector. Müller has publicity value. Which can be a decided handicap to ourselves, as we discovered in the case of Eichmann.'

'And if you never catch him?'

I was interested in Doctor Lazarus. It seemed to me that he would never rest in peace, that his life's work could never be done.

He looked at me thoughtfully, weighing what answer he should give me.

'I take it, Inspector, that you believe in the justice of God?'

'I do. I am, however, a paid professional servant of a very inadequate, pathetically incompetent human justice.'

'My answer to your question might well be your answer, Inspector.'

'I might – possibly – answer that I did not know – nor could I know – what punishments – human punishments – have visited such a man.'

'And have you developed that argument?'

'It is neither my task nor my right.'

'Nor mine.'


I thought on the way home that Doctor Lazarus had spent years in the camps. He was a doctor of medicine, and of parapsychology. He knew a great deal about law. And he knew what it was like to have no person left in the world. He would be quite an expert on punishments.

Whereas I was a bum inspector of police, an expert on asking rag-and-bone men to show their pushcart licences. An expert, perhaps, on rag-and-bone men.

I couldn't eat my dinner.

I couldn't explain to Arlette.

I opened a drawer, strapped on a shoulder-holster, put a pistol in it, shrugged my shoulders and put the whole lot back.

I thought of everybody I knew. I know a Jewish doctor who is a neurologist – I know the Procureur-Général – I know a few retired policemen – I have read a lot of books; some of them by writers who know a good deal about people. I stared at my bookshelves. Mauriac, Simenon, Flaubert, Charles de Foucauld, Saint Teresa, Büchner, Dostoyevski, Racine, the Memorial of Saint Helena.

Either there weren't enough books, or I hadn't read them properly. Nobody could help me, not even Arlette.

I muttered something at her, took a tram to the Central Station, and got on a train that smelt very nasty indeed, of stale cheap cigarsmoke and imperfectly washed humanity that has a prejudice against open windows.

I thought about Corneille and Oliver Cromwell.

The only person I could think of in the whole world who might be able to help me was SS Lieutenant-General

Heinrich Müller. Whose grave was in Berlin. Written on it: 'To our beloved father'.

Doctor Lazarus, or one of his friends, had come along busily looking at bones and said the back teeth were wrong. Anyway the bones of several people were in the grave.

Perhaps Mr Müller had had no objection at the time to company.


# 6


In Drente it was dry, and the night air felt warm, with a gentle westerly breeze. I had the idea the sun had been shining all day. That was all wrong. It was supposed to get warmer as one went south and nearer the sea – and in Amsterdam the streets had been full of greasy half-frozen slush, the air at or below freezing point, and the sky trying hard either to snow or to rain and achieving neither, just a foul misty mizzle.

I walked from the station, in Zwinderen. Nobody looked at me. I got to the lunatic asylum and wondered whether they'd been brave enough to put Burger there. No such luck probably; they were more likely to keep her havering for months, poor bitch, in the House of Keeping in Assen.

I rang at the gate and pretty soon I heard the slow, shuffling, but still firm footstep across the brick path. The eyes glanced through the gap in the barricade; when they saw me a great jump of the nerves went across the whole face like electricity; a spark that penetrated the powerful facial muscles, the dark glasses, all the insulation.

'Forgive me; I failed for a second to recognize you. But come in. Pleasant surprise. I suppose there is some detail that has been forgotten, that you have posted back to fill in a few more forms?'

He was talking too much too.

'That's about it,' vaguely.

I sat down in the accustomed place, the creaky cane arm-chair. Besançon sat at his desk, hands folded in his lap, head and shoulders bowed. Like that, he was an insignificant little man.

I had no idea what to say; a silence grew that was almost as complete as the one I had broken into.

'A detail,' I said at last with an effort, 'that must be repaired. I am often very stupid.'

'I have never yet had that impression.'

'You don't know me that well, General,' I said in German. It was funny: I had a sort of embarrassment. I was unable to say straight out – 'You are a notorious man; the execrated, the fearful, the larger-than-life.' Quite right. This was not any of those things. This was an ageing, tired, frightened, dying man.

'Your German has a Hamburg sound, it seems to me.'

'I was stationed there – nearly a year. In nineteen forty-five. It's not good.'

'I understand what you say, well enough.'

'I thought you would.'

He straightened his shoulders, lifted his head; I began to recognize the man I knew more. The voice got its timbre back, its sardonic tone.

'I would like only to disclaim the General. Napoleon created Marshals of France and the Empire; they were right to keep their titles. I have never had the slightest use for this one. Since at last, apparently, I have a name, use it.'

'I might, if I knew what to say.'

'You came, I take it, to do, not just to say.'

'I don't know what to do, either.'

He looked at me. He got up then, shuffled slowly across the room – I could see he missed his stick – and brought his brandy bottle and two glasses. He offered one to me; I took it. We clinked together solemnly, two men separated by everything and by nothing.

'You're drinking, then?' I said stupidly.

'I am forbidden alcohol, yes. What importance has it? I shall not in any case live long.'

I suddenly got an extremely silly idea, which startled me.

'This brandy's not poisoned, is it?' It got his ironical smile.

'I had thought my melodramatic days over. I possess no poisons. I have no wish to kill myself; I have no interest even in killing you.'

'Yet I have told no one I was coming here.' Did I wish to tempt him, I wondered. Why did I say that?

'I think I understand that.'

'I dare say that I could, quite easily, disappear. Not even my wife knows where I am.'

'Are you suggesting that I should disappear?'

'Would it help?'

'No longer.'

'You'd rather go in front of a tribunal?'

'At least I should not defend myself with excuses. Like Eichmann. The eternal subordinate. The man was always, you know, something of a fool. A competent fool.'

'I don't think it ever occurred to anyone to bother whether he was a fool,' I said, perhaps too sarcastically.

'Is that what you propose doing? To hand me to the Jews? Whom I persecuted, killed? Whose identity, finally, I stole? It would be more than just.'

'I don't want to be more than just. And I must not be less.'

'You simply don't know,' looking straight at me.

'No.'

'Why?'

'I don't think I should ever understand. Even if you told me. I don't want any confessions. I could not grasp it. You have done things that are monstrous, unbelievable. Legend has exaggerated your exploits to a degree where I can't take them seriously. I can only see you as you are. A retired civil servant with a nervous illness. A man I have known, spoken to, shaken hands with, clinked glasses with. A man I like. Or is that Besançon?'

'Perhaps,' gravely.

'I should prefer to have had none of these experiences.'

'I understand.'

'The real Besançon, I take it . . .'

'Is buried in the grave in Berlin.'

'He resembled you closely?'

'Very. Looking at us together, one could not tell which was the Jew. Bormann made a coarse joke about it one day.'

'You had planned it for a long time?'

'I planned,' impassively, 'to steal him. Which I did.'

'Your family knows?'

'No.'

I left it at that.

'It was noticed, here, that you shunned the company of women. It was thought by some a suspicious circumstance.'

He laughed, quite ordinarily, pleasantly.

'Why do you laugh?'

'I had told myself, you see, that I would keep a sort of fidelity to my wife. I was – I am – what is called a good family man. That, it seems, has drawn attention to me. When I had no other fidelities . . . neither to myself, to my country, to my state, to my function, to my absurd Leader. To nothing.' He held his open hands up as though to show me that they contained nothing. He laid them then on the table, flat, loose, watching the trembling with a sort of curiosity.

It was good French cognac. Written on the label was *Fournisseur à Sa Majesté le Roi de Suède.* He had given me a generous glass too. Perhaps it gave me false courage.

'Tell me, then. What did you do?'

'What happens to civil servants, Inspector van der Valk, who come to the conclusion that their government has betrayed them? They commit treason. Himmler, that idealist, tried to bargain with the Americans. I was more clear-sighted. I had understood the meaning of Yalta, of Casablanca. Germans alone could save Germany. I was too late; we had committed too many crimes.'

I do believe he had forgotten I was there. He had passed into his familiar train of thought, from which there was no outlet. He had perhaps been mad – he was no longer so, and he doubted whether it ever had been so. He had deceived himself with mass hysteria, and remained too clear-sighted to believe in it. He had taken refuge in the peculiar German cloudiness and confusion of thought that accompany German orderliness and efficiency, and found his thought refused to cloud; the merciful opacity of Himmler had eluded him. Everything had failed him, one refuge after the other. The mystique of the Administration, of the Fatherland, of the Leader – all had crumbled and collapsed.

He had looked for every possible excuse. When he had seen what crimes he had committed in the name of his sacred Department he had tried to quieten his torments by embarking on wilder, more fantastic, more dreadful crimes than ever. He had fallen into the myth of predestination, believing – for a while – that he had been sent as a scourge, himself damned, but elected by God to lie heavy on the necks of his fellow men.

He had clung to every excuse as long as he had been able. His clear mind had forced him inexorably to abandon one after the other.

Finally he had found himself the most odious name in Europe; every human being alert for the blood of Gestapo Müller. All his intelligence and force had been called up to save his pride. What did they know; what could they understand, these peasants? Americans, English, Russians – his contempt for them was as great as had been his contempt for Germans, for Jews. He was not going to defend himself, justify himself. And he wasn't going to be caught, to be ignominiously butchered. God would save Müller. God had. Ever since he had wondered why.

Instead of death, and possible expiation, peace, he had been allowed to live. He disdained the network of underground sympathizers. Fools and criminals.

He did not dare even to trust his family. God had sent him a slow, mortal disease, as though to say to him, 'You have still time'. But God had not affected his intelligence.

'A man will cling to his life,' I heard myself saying.

'I agree. Even Müller. During the long periods of interrogation I thought daily that I would be discovered. How many times have I wanted to scream, to say, "Fools, fools, can you not see what is under your nose?" They accepted me as a Jew. For years I stayed here, wondering what was required of me. Then the police came again. Not to demand a reckoning from Müller, but to know whether a crazy old Jew had written obscene letters to respectable Dutch housewives. The irony of it . . . I lived in daily fear, but I clung still to my life. It is all I have left. It is worth remarkably little. You have come to take it. You are the one who, accidentally, has discovered the secret that all Europe has hunted for.'

I did not care for the idea that I was the instrument chosen by God to bring Gestapo Müller to justice. What justice? Justice, with somebody who has committed crimes like these, does not exist. They put Eichmann in a glass case, and played out a long-drawn, odious, humiliating farce. It did the Jews no good, the world no good. Did it do Eichmann good? It was not my job to decide that. They had to hang him; they had no choice. What battle had gone on in the mind of the President of Israel, before with a sigh he had signed the paper that released the trap-door?

I was furious with the chance – chance? – that had brought me face to face with this man. Surely he was coming to the inescapable conclusion that what was wanted of him was a voluntary surrender to a will that was not his.

Free will is the most important thing we have. I refuse to be a predestined agent for the arrest of Müller.

'Damn you,' I said. 'I should take you outside and shoot you, with no more ado than if you were a sheep-killing dog.'

'That is quite natural,' he said in Besançon's voice.

'Both dramatic and handy,' I said sourly. I was not happy at my seeming inability to do anything at all.

'You are a bad policeman,' thoughtfully, wearily.

'I have never realized it more completely than now.'

'We have at least self-knowledge in common. I will help you, by telling you a story.'

'Go ahead,' dully.

'It was decided to provoke a frontier incident that would give pretext for an invasion of Poland. A man called Müller was entrusted with this. He gave the operation the name "Canned Goods" – being a fellow of humour. He arranged for half a dozen condemned criminals to be transported to a selected border post where there was a communications centre of no importance. The criminals were given injections, dressed in German uniforms, and shot while unconscious, to give the impression of a Polish attack.' He paused, and gave me a smile that belonged to Müller – the Müller that thought of the name 'Canned Goods' – rather than to Besançon.

'I have had no injection, of course. But I am dying as surely as though I had. And I am a condemned criminal.'

I found my hands trembling. Like his. If I had a gun, I thought, I would shoot this man, here, on the spot. Who would ever know?

He reached down slowly, opened the drawer of his table, and put a pistol on the desk between us. I stared at this pistol.

'I took considerable pains to acquire that. I have often been tempted to use it. But I have had too much pride.'

The tension broke; I felt myself a man again.

'You Germans. Always a drama.'

'You are a policeman. It would be easily arranged.'

'And would it satisfy your conscience for "Canned Goods"? Your life is no good to me. Yes, I thought the trials at Nuremberg a farce. I would have shot them straight away, "while trying to escape" – the classic formula. But I can't shoot you.'

'You are going to let me go? To die my lingering little death, reading the Bible every day?'

'I have to decide.'

'What do you believe?' he asked suddenly.

'Do not ask me what I believe.'

'I am a better policeman than you are, Mr van der Valk.'

'Perhaps,' I said. 'We shall see.'

Fear suddenly passed over the face again, despite the self-control.

'You are going to arrest me.'

'That is my duty.'

The hand went suddenly to the pistol, but the degenerated nerves were too unsure. I released the grip, put the catch on, and stuck the thing in my pocket.

'Put your overcoat on.'

'You're going to give me to the Jews.'

'I'm going to give you to the government of the Kingdom of the Netherlands. No Jews will kidnap you.'

'I see no difference,' bitterly. 'You take refuge under your official identity – I thought you were a man. Your kingdom will do the same. Officially, praiseworthily, they will give me to the Jews. You ... bureaucrat. Without the courage either to let me go or shoot me.'

'Listen to me.' My voice, I could hear, was not under control. 'Every instinct I have is to let you go. Moral, ethical, legal, personal – call it what you like; I don't care. And it would be expedient into the bargain. I won't do it.'

I watched him bring his features under control.

'Very well,' said the old voice, with its calm, quiet tone. 'I had all the same reasons to surrender myself – and I could not do that, either. You are right to force me.' It had dignity. For the first time, I felt my old liking, even respect, for the man.

'I will get my coat.' He turned to me again. 'I have courage, you know.'

We walked, the old man using his rubber-tipped stick. We passed the Jewish cemetery. Müller glanced up at the Hebrew characters on the gateposts.

'You know what it says?'

'I can't read Hebrew.'

'I can,' softly. 'One of Müller's strange accomplishments. It says "Born, mankind is doomed to die. Dead, mankind is destined to live again".'

We walked on.

'Grace,' suddenly. 'Oliver Cromwell fought his hardest battles for it. A crowning mercy . . .'

'I don't believe,' I said, 'that grace has to be fought for. I believe it's there for the asking.'

We reached the police bureau.

The desk man recognized me this time; he got up. Seeing Besançon, he looked puzzled. What had they arrested Burger for, then?

'This man is to be given a cell. I want him treated with every consideration. There's no charge, at present.'

'But what am I to put on the form, Inspector?'

'Oh, some stupid bureaucratic phrase. "Provisional detention pending judicial decision" – never mind, I'll do it. Here, give me the keys.'

The fellow looked bemused, but wasn't going to question an officer. I opened the steel door. The bureau was a modern one, and the cell was clean and well kept.

'Say nothing here – you'll understand. I'll see about changing this as soon as I possibly can. In the meantime, I'll see that you get everything you need from your home.'

The old man was trembling badly, shakier than I had

ever seen him. But the eyes – the famous darting eyes of legend – were steady. He looked very resolute.

'Thank you.'

I wheeled abruptly at the door.

'Forgive me,' I held out my hand.

'You are willing to shake hands with Heinrich Müller?'

'Yes.'

He pulled himself up, and gave me a formal, German bow.

'I'll phone your Inspector,' I said to the desk man, who was fussing about Christian names and Date and Place of Birth. 'No – I'd better go round to his house.'

'Safety of the Realm Act?'

'I've no idea myself. If I were you I'd just say and do nothing, till you hear. I'll make a personal report to the Procureur-Général tomorrow morning. He'll decide.'

'But my god, Van der Valk – who is it?'

'SS Lieutenant-General Heinrich Müller.'

It made a good exit line.

# 7

'Inspector van der Valk, Central Recherche, requests an interview with Mr Sailer.'

'You mean this morning?'

'It is extremely urgent. I can't put that strongly enough.'

'I'll see what I can do,' rather astonished. 'Will you wait?'

'Yes.'

'Mr Sailer will see you now.'

'Ah. Van der Valk. Good morning. This is rather unusual. I take it a request of this sort is not made without grave reason?'

'Very grave, sir. I need your advice, and I need your help.'

'You have committed an imprudence?'

'No sir. But I have done something from which I shall never be quite free.'

'Connected with this affair in Drente?'

'There are two affairs, sir. The first was simple – I have a report for you here, that I would have sent over by messenger this morning. But the other . . .'

'A grave affair?'

'Yes. And a headline – in every newspaper in the world.'

'I am at your service. That, among other things, is what I am here for.'

'At its briefest – I have, while in Drente, discovered, identified and arrested Gestapo Müller. He's in detention – no charge on the form, and under his assumed name – in the local bureau. I have notified the local inspector – he doesn't know what to do any more than I did. He agreed to wait until I had made a verbal report.'

Mr Sailer considered, in silence, my rather hysterical words.

'Nobody, Van der Valk, need envy an incumbent of this chair. Very well. You had better relate me your tale in detail.'


'. . . And for these reasons, and the fact that I know I am not altogether fitted for my responsibilities, I would like to offer my resignation. That's all, sir.'

There was a very long silence. Mr Sailer's head was upright, but his eyes rested on his hands, which were loosely clasped, upon his blotter. He raised them slowly; they stayed on me. I tried to meet them the way Müller had met mine.

'Nothing can alter the course of the law,' very quietly.

'I can't argue with you, sir. I certainly can't query a judicial opinion of yours. But if I'm no longer a policeman, I could say that the law makes no provision for a man like that. As a man – even as a policeman – I can say that no man expiates crimes like that. Any way at all. It's something needed from the whole human race.'

'Go on.'

But I had lost my grip on myself.

'I can't help it. He's only a man. Not only because I talked to him, shook hands with him, liked him even. Ach, I'm no good for this job. He even said so himself – a fellow that knows something about policemen.'

'That'll do.' There was another long pause. Mr Sailer was making up his mind.

'You have earned respect by what you have done. And personally, I admire you.

'A bad policeman – you will please allow your superiors to judge of that. Mr Müller's superiors' – in the voice like desert sand for which Sailer was known – 'appear to have found him useful, but we would not – nor, I think, would they – recommend him as a textbook model.

'Your responsibility does not reach as far as a case which, as you pointed out, has not been imagined, for which no provision has been made in the Criminal Code, for which there are no precedents in jurisprudence. Your conscience is not an official concern, nor is it mine. You have behaved with scrupulous exactitude in acting as you have and in making – shall I call it a confession? – to me. I approve your movements, unhesitatingly.

'This responsibility is now mine. You may have a confidence in exchange for your own: I will endeavour to apply moral principles to my decision in this matter – as you did. The matter is from this moment out of your hands.'

Another pause, shorter.

'Your resignation is refused. The State of the Netherlands, embodied at this instant in myself, will not accept the loss of a responsible public servant for the motives you have given me.'

Mr Sailer leaned forward slightly. His small healthy eyes impaled me.

'I will recommend your promotion within a short term. In particular, your transfer to a department where, I think, your qualities will find use. I am thinking of the juvenile branch.

'Lastly, I have, this morning, received a letter from the burgomaster of Zwinderen. He speaks of you in high terms, and sees fit to inform me that you were of personal service to himself in a situation placing a public official in a difficult position. I have, I think, no more to say. Have you?'

'No sir.'

'I have no doubt but that Mr Tak has plenty for you to do . . . You can leave your written report here.'


There is in Holland a comic strip – the drawings are good, and the text original, witty, sharp in grasp of character; a comic strip with character; that is very rare. It concerns a very stupid, snobbish, pleasant bear whose name is Olivier B. Bommel. He is a nice fellow, very aristocratic. He lives in a castle called Schloss Bommelstein, where he has a butler who is an excellent cook. And, by sacred tradition, a Bommel adventure must always end with a festive, abundant dinner.

Arlette, who goes rather far, says that Bommel is the only readable literature in Holland; I have often been inclined to agree. I agree with the tradition, too. When I went home, quite as stupid and bewildered as Bommel ever is, Arlette had a very famous country dish: boiled ham with the four purées – apples, potatoes, celery and flageolet beans.

I did not tell her I had wanted to resign. Nor anything about General Müller. What would have been the point? Because I had not slept last night, should she not be allowed to sleep tonight?

It would have been a waste, too, of a good dinner. And my free weekend.

'We seem to have got quite a hurrah letter from the burgomaster. And there was a hint that I may be promoted after all. There's a vacancy in the juvenile branch; I've been told it's me – unofficially. Post has rank of chief inspector. Good, hm?'

'Oh, darling. Where could we go on holiday when you get a rise?'

'Anyway, not beautiful Drente, wouldn't you agree?'

'It wasn't that bad,' said Arlette, '– looking back, I quite enjoyed myself.'